THE FULL CUPBOARD OF LIFE

THE FULL CUPBOARD OF LIFE

Alexander McCall Smith

Alfred A. Knopf Canada

PUBLISHED BY ALFRED A. KNOPF CANADA

Copyright © 2003 Alexander McCall Smith

All rights reserved under International and Pan-American Copyright Conventions. Published in 2004 by Alfred A. Knopf Canada, a division of Random House of Canada Limited, Toronto, and simultaneously by Pantheon Books, a division of Random House, Inc., New York. Originally published in Great Britain by Polygon, an imprint of Birlinn, Ltd., Edinburgh, in 2003. Distributed by Random House of Canada Limited, Toronto.

Knopf Canada and colophon are trademarks.

National Library of Canada Cataloguing in Publication
McCall Smith, R. A.
The full cupboard of life : more from the No. 1 Ladies' Detective Agency /
Alexander McCall Smith.

ISBN 0-676-97570-4

I. Title.

PR6063.C326F84 2004   823'.914   C2003-905924-3

First Edition

www.randomhouse.ca

Printed and bound in the United States of America

2 4 6 8 9 7 5 3 1

This book is for
Soula Ross
and
Vicky Taylor

THE FULL CUPBOARD OF LIFE

_____

CHAPTER ONE

A GREAT SADNESS AMONG
THE CARS OF BOTSWANA

PRECIOUS RAMOTSWE was sitting at her desk at the No. 1 Ladies' Detective Agency in Gaborone. From where she sat she could gaze out of the window, out beyond the acacia trees, over the grass and the scrub bush, to the hills in their blue haze of heat. It was such a noble country, and so wide, stretching for mile upon mile to brown horizons at the very edge of Africa. It was late summer, and there had been good rains that year. This was important, as good rains meant productive fields, and productive fields meant large, ripened pumpkins of the sort that traditionally built ladies like Mma Ramotswe so enjoyed eating. The yellow flesh of a pumpkin or a squash, boiled and then softened with a lump of butter (if one's budget stretched to that), was one of God's greatest gifts to Botswana. And it tasted so good, too, with a slice of fine Botswana beef, dripping in gravy.

Oh yes, God had given a great deal to Botswana, as she had been told all those years ago at Sunday school in Mochudi. "Write a list of Botswana's heavenly blessings," the teacher had said. And the young Mma Ramotswe, chewing on the end of her indelible pencil, and feeling the sun bearing down on the tin roof of the Sunday school, heat so insistent that the tin creaked in protest against its restraining bolts, had written: (*1*) *the land*; (*2*) *the people who live on the land*; (*3*) *the animals, and specially the fat cattle*. She had stopped at that, but, after a pause, had added: (*4*) *the railway line from Lobatse to Francistown*. This list, once submitted for approval, had come back with a large blue tick after each item, and the comment written in: *Well done, Precious! You are a sensible girl. You have correctly shown why Botswana is a fortunate country.*

And this was quite true. Mma Ramotswe was indeed a sensible person and Botswana was a fortunate country. When Botswana had become independent all those years ago, on that heart-stilling night when the fireworks failed to be lit on time, and when the dusty wind had seemed to augur only ill, there had been so little. There were only three secondary schools for the whole country, a few clinics, and a measly eight miles of tarred road. That was all. But was it? Surely there was a great deal more than that. There was a country so large that the land seemed to have no limits; there was a sky so wide and so free that the spirit could rise and soar and not feel in the least constrained; and there were the people, the quiet, patient people, who had survived in this land, and who loved it. Their tenacity was rewarded, because underneath the land there were the diamonds, and the cattle prospered, and brick by brick the people built a country of which anybody could be proud. That was what Botswana had, and that is why it was a fortunate country.

Mma Ramotswe had founded the No. 1 Ladies' Detective Agency by selling the cattle left her by her father, Obed Ramotswe, a good man whom everybody respected. And for this reason she made sure that his picture was on the office wall, alongside, but slightly lower than, the picture of the late President of Botswana, Sir Seretse Khama, paramount chief of the Bangwato, founding president of Botswana, and gentleman. The last of these attributes was perhaps the most important in Mma Ramotswe's eyes. A man could be a hereditary ruler, or an elected president, but not be a gentleman, and that would show in his every deed. But if you had a leader who was a gentleman, with all that this meant, then you were lucky indeed. And Botswana had been very lucky in that respect, because all three of her presidents had been good men, gentlemen, who were modest in their bearing, as a gentleman should be. One day, perhaps, a woman might become president, and Mma Ramotswe thought that this would be even better, provided, of course, that the lady in question had the right qualities of modesty and caution. Not all ladies had those qualities, Mma Ramotswe reflected; some of them being quite conspicuously lacking in that respect.

Take that woman who was always on the radio—a political woman who was always telling people what to do. She had an irritating voice, like that of a jackal, and a habit of flirting with men in a shameless way, provided that the men in question could do something to advance her career. If they could not, then they were ignored. Mma Ramotswe had seen this happening; she had seen her ignoring the Bishop at a public function, in order to talk to an important government minister who might put in a good word for her in the right place. It had been transparent. Bishop Theophilus had opened his mouth to say something about the rain and she had said, "Yes, Bishop, yes. Rain is very important." But even as she spoke, she was looking in the direction of the minister, and smiling at him. After a few minutes, she had slipped away, leaving the Bishop behind, and sidled up to the minister to whisper something to him. Mma Ramotswe, who had watched the whole thing, was in no doubt about what that something had been, for she knew women of this sort and there were many of them. So they would have to be careful before choosing a woman as president. It would have to be the right sort of woman; a woman who knew what hard work was and what it was like to bear half the world upon your shoulders.

On that day, sitting at her desk, Mma Ramotswe allowed her thoughts to wander. There was nothing in particular to do. There were no outstanding matters to investigate, as she had just completed a major enquiry on behalf of a large store that suspected, but could not prove, that one of its senior staff was embezzling money. Its accountants had looked at the books and had found discrepancies, but had been unable to find how and where the money had disappeared. In his frustration at the continuing losses, the managing director had called in Mma Ramotswe, who had compiled a list of all the senior staff and had decided to look into their circumstances. If money was disappearing, then there was every likelihood that somebody at the other end would be spending it. And this elementary conclusion—so obvious really— had led her straight to the culprit. It was not that he had advertised his ill-gotten wealth; Mma Ramotswe had been obliged to elicit this information by placing temptation before each suspect. At length, one had succumbed to the prospect of an expensive bargain and had been able to offer payment in cash—a sum beyond the means of a person in such a position. It was not the sort of investigation which she enjoyed, because it involved recrimination and shame, and Mma Ramotswe preferred to forgive, if at all possible. "I am a forgiving lady," she said, which was true. She did forgive, even to the extent of bearing no grudge against Note Mokoti, her cruel former husband, who had caused her such suffering during their brief, ill-starred marriage. She had forgiven Note, even though she did not see him any more, and she would tell him that he was forgiven if he came to her now. Why, she asked herself, why keep a wound open when forgiveness can close it?

Her unhappiness with Note had convinced her that she

would never marry again. But then, on that extraordinary evening some time ago, when Mr J.L.B. Matekoni had proposed to her after he had spent all afternoon fixing the dispirited engine of her tiny white van, she had accepted him. And that was the right decision, for Mr J.L.B. Matekoni was not only the best mechanic in Botswana, but he was one of the kindest and most gracious of men. Mr J.L.B. Matekoni would do anything for one who needed help, and, in a world of increasing dishonesty, he still practised the old Botswana morality. He was a good man, which, when all is said and done, is the finest thing that you can say about any man. He was a good man.

It was strange at first to be an engaged lady; a status somewhere between spinsterhood and marriage; committed to another, but not yet another's spouse. Mma Ramotswe had imagined that they would marry within six months of the engagement, but that time had passed, and more, and still Mr J.L.B. Matekoni had said nothing about a wedding. Certainly he had bought her a ring and had spoken freely, and proudly, of her as his fiancée, but nothing had been said about the date of the wedding. She still kept her house in Zebra Drive, and he lived in his house in the Village, near the old Botswana Defence Force Club and the clinic, and not far from the old graveyard. Some people, of course, did not like to live too close to a graveyard, but modern people, like Mma Ramotswe, said that this was nonsense. Indeed, there were many differences of opinion here. The people who lived around Tlokweng, the Batlokwa, had a custom of burying their ancestors in a small, mud-walled round house, a rondavel, in the yard. This meant that those members of the family who died were always there with you, which was a good practice, thought Mma Ramotswe. If a mother died, then she might be buried under the hut of the children, so that her spirit could watch over them. That must have been comforting for children, thought Mma

Ramotswe, to have the mother under the stamped cattle-dung floor.

There were many good things about the old ways, and it made Mma Ramotswe sad to think that some of these ways were dying out. Botswana had been a special country, and still was, but it had been more special in the days when everybody—or almost everybody—observed the old Botswana ways. The modern world was selfish, and full of cold and rude people. Botswana had never been like that, and Mma Ramotswe was determined that her small corner of Botswana, which was the house on Zebra Drive, and the office that the No. 1 Ladies' Detective Agency and Tlokweng Road Speedy Motors shared, would always remain part of the old Botswana, where people greeted one another politely and listened to what others had to say, and did not shout or think just of themselves. That would never happen in that little part of Botswana, ever.

That morning, sitting at her desk, a steaming mug of bush tea before her, Mma Ramotswe was alone with her thoughts. It was nine o'clock, which was well into the working morning (which started at seven-thirty), but Mma Makutsi, her assistant, had been instructed to go to the post office on her way to work and would not arrive for a little while yet. Mma Makutsi had been hired as a secretary, but had quickly proved her value and had been promoted to assistant detective. In addition to this, she was Assistant Manager of Tlokweng Road Speedy Motors, a role which she had taken on with conspicuous success when Mr J.L.B. Matekoni had been ill. Mma Ramotswe was lucky to have such an assistant; there were many lazy secretaries in Gaborone, who sat in the security of their jobs tapping at a keyboard from time to time or occasionally picking up the telephone. Most of these lazy secretaries answered the telephone in the same tone of voice, as if the cares of being a secretary were overwhelming and there was nothing that they could possibly do for the caller. Mma Makutsi was quite unlike these; indeed she answered the telephone rather too enthusiastically, and had sometimes scared callers away altogether. But this was a minor fault in one who brought with her the distinction of being the most accomplished graduate of her year from the Botswana Secretarial College, where she had scored ninety-seven per cent in the final examinations.

As Mma Ramotswe sat at her desk, she heard sounds of activity from the garage on the other side of the building. Mr J.L.B. Matekoni was at work with his two apprentices, young men who seemed entirely obsessed with girls and who were always leaving grease marks about the building. Around each light switch, in spite of many exhortations and warnings, there was an area of black discolouration, where the apprentices had placed their dirty fingers. And Mma Ramotswe had even found greasy fingerprints on her telephone receiver and, more irritatingly still, on the door of the stationery cupboard.

"Mr J.L.B. Matekoni provides towels and all that lint for wiping off grease," she had said to the older apprentice. "They are always there in the washroom. When you have finished working on a car, wash your hands before you touch other things. What is so hard about that?"

"I always do that," said the apprentice. "It is not fair to talk to me like that, Mma. I am a very clean mechanic."

"Then is it you?" asked Mma Ramotswe, turning to the younger apprentice.

"I am very clean too, Mma," he said. "I am always washing my hands. Always. Always."

"Then it must be me," said Mma Ramotswe. "I must be the one with greasy hands. It must be me or Mma Makutsi. Maybe we get greasy from opening letters."

The older apprentice appeared to think about this for a moment. "Maybe," he said.

"There's very little point in trying to talk to them," Mr J.L.B. Matekoni had observed when Mma Ramotswe subsequently told him of this conversation. "There is something missing in their brains. Sometimes I think it is a large part, as big as a carburettor maybe."

Now Mma Ramotswe heard the sound of voices coming from the garage. Mr J.L.B. Matekoni was saying something to the apprentices, and then there came a mumbling sound as one of the young men answered. Another voice; this time raised; it was Mr J.L.B. Matekoni.

Mma Ramotswe listened. They had done something again, and he was reprimanding them, which was unusual. Mr J.L.B. Matekoni was a mild man, who did not like conflict, and always spoke politely. If he felt it necessary to raise his voice, then it must have been something very annoying indeed.

"Diesel fuel in an ordinary engine," he said, as he entered her office, wiping his hands on a large piece of lint. "Would you believe it, Mma Ramotswe? That . . . that silly boy, the younger one, put diesel fuel into the tank of a non-diesel vehicle. Now we have to drain everything out and try to clean the thing up."

"I'm sorry," said Mma Ramotswe. "But I am not surprised." She paused for a moment. "What will happen to them? What will happen when they are working somewhere else—somewhere where there is no longer a kind person like you to watch over them?"

Mr J.L.B. Matekoni shrugged. "They will ruin cars left, right, and centre," he said. "That is what will happen to them. There will be great sadness among the cars of Botswana."

Mma Ramotswe shook her head. Then, on a sudden impulse,

and without thinking at all why she should say this, she asked, "And what will happen to us, Mr J.L.B. Matekoni?"

The words were out, and Mma Ramotswe looked down at her hands on the desk, and at the diamond ring, which looked back up at her. She had said it, and Mr J.L.B. Matekoni had heard what she had said.

Mr J.L.B. Matekoni looked surprised. "Why do you ask, Mma? What do you mean when you ask what will happen to us?"

Mma Ramotswe raised her eyes. She thought that she might as well continue, now that she had begun. "I was wondering what would happen to us. I was wondering whether we would ever get married, or whether we would continue to be engaged people for the rest of our lives. I was just wondering, that was all."

Mr J.L.B. Matekoni stood quite still. "But we are engaged to be married," he said. "That means that we will get married. Everybody knows that."

Mma Ramotswe sighed. "Yes, but now they are saying: when will those two get married? That is what they are all saying. And maybe I should say that too."

For a few moments Mr J.L.B. Matekoni said nothing. He continued to wipe his hands on the lint, as if concentrating on a delicate task, and then he spoke. "We will get married next year. That is the best thing to do. By then we will have made all the arrangements and saved enough money for a big wedding. Weddings cost a lot, you know. Maybe it will be next year, or the year after that, but we shall certainly get married. There is no doubt about that."

"But I have got money in the Standard Chartered Bank," said Mma Ramotswe. "I could use that or I could sell some cattle. I still have some cattle that my father left me. They have multiplied. I have almost two hundred now."

"You must not sell cattle," said Mr J.L.B. Matekoni. "It is good to keep cattle. We must wait."

He stared at her, almost reproachfully, and Mma Ramotswe looked away. The subject was too awkward, too raw, to be discussed openly, and so she did not pursue the matter. It seemed as if he was frightened of marriage, which must be the reason why he was proving so slow to commit himself. Well, there were men like that; nice men who were fond enough of women but who were wary of getting married. If that was the case, then she would be realistic about it and continue to be an engaged lady. It was not a bad situation to be in, after all; indeed, there were some arguments for preferring an engagement to a marriage. You often heard of difficult husbands, but how often did you hear of difficult fiancés? The answer to that, thought Mma Ramotswe, was never.

Mr J.L.B. Matekoni left the room, and Mma Ramotswe picked up her mug of bush tea. If she was going to remain an engaged lady, then she would make the most of it, and one of the ways to do this would be to enjoy her free time. She would read a bit more and spend more time on her shopping. And she might also join a club of some sort, if she could find one, or perhaps even form one herself, perhaps something like a Cheerful Ladies' Club, a club for ladies in whose lives there was some sort of gap—in her case a gap of waiting—but who were determined to make the most of their time. It was a sentiment of which her father, the late Obed Ramotswe, would have approved; her father, that good man who had always used his time to good effect and who was always in her thoughts, as constantly and supportively as if he were buried under the floor directly beneath her.

CHAPTER TWO

HOW TO RUN AN ORPHAN FARM

MMA SILVIA POTOKWANE, the matron of the orphan farm, was sorting out bits of carpeting for a jumble sale. The pieces of carpet were scattered about the ground under a large syringa tree, and she and several of the housemothers were busy placing them in order of desirability. The carpets were not old at all, but were off-cuts which had been donated by a flooring firm in Gaborone. At the end of every job, no matter how careful the carpet layers were, there would always be odd pieces which simply did not fit. Sometimes these were quite large, if the end of a roll had been used, or the room had been a particularly awkward shape. But none of them was square or rectangular, and this meant that their usefulness was limited.

"Nobody has a room this shape," said one of the housemothers, drawing Mma Potokwane's attention to a triangular piece of flecked red carpet. "I do not know what we can do with this."

Mma Potokwane bent down to examine the carpet. It was not easy for her to bend, as she was an unusually traditional shape. She enjoyed her food, certainly, but she was also very active, and one might have thought that all that walking about the orphan farm, peering into every corner just to keep everybody on their toes, would have shed the pounds, but it had not. All the women in her family had been that build, and it had brought them good fortune and success; there was no point, she felt, being a thin and unhappy person when the attractions of being a comfortable person were so evident. And men liked women like that too. It was a terrible thing that the outside world had done to Africa, bringing in the idea that slender ladies, some as thin as a sebokoldi, a millipede, should be considered desirable. That was not what men really wanted. Men wanted women whose shape reminded them of good things on the table.

"It is a very strange shape," agreed Mma Potokwane. "But if you put together two triangles, then do you not get a square, or something quite close to a square? Do you not think that is true, Mma?"

The housemother looked blank for a moment, but then the wisdom of Mma Potokwane's suggestion dawned upon her and she smiled broadly. There were other triangular pieces, and she now reached for one of these, and held it in position alongside the awkward red piece. The result was an almost perfect square, even if the two pieces of carpet were a different colour.

Mma Potokwane was pleased with the result. Once they had sorted out the carpets, they would put up a notice in the Tlokweng Community Centre and invite people to a carpet sale. They would have no difficulty in selling everything, she thought, and the money would go into the fund that they were building up for book prizes for the children. At the end of each term, those who had done well would receive a prize for their efforts; an atlas, perhaps, or a Setswana Bible, or some other book which would be useful at school. Although she was not a great reader, Mma Potokwane was a firm believer in the power of the book. The more books that Botswana had, in her view, the better. It would be on books that the future would be based; books and the people who knew how to use them.

It would be wonderful, she thought, to write a book which would help other people. In her case, she would never have the time to do it, and even if she had the time, then she very much doubted whether she would have the necessary ability. But if she were to write a book, then the title would undoubtedly be *How to Run an Orphan Farm*. That would be a useful book for whomever took over from her when she retired, or indeed for the many other ladies who ran orphan farms elsewhere. Mma Potokwane had spent some time thinking about the contents of such a work. There would be a great deal about the ordinary day-to-day business of an orphan farm: the arranging of meals, the sorting out of duties and so on. But there would also be a chapter on the psychology which went into running an orphan farm. Mma Potokwane knew a great deal about that. She could tell you, for example, of the importance of keeping brothers and sisters together, if at all possible, and of how to deal with behavioural problems. These were almost always due to insecurity and had one cure and one cure alone: love. That, at least, had been her experience, and even if the message was a simple one, it was, in her view, utterly true.

Another chapter—a very important one—would be on fund raising. Every orphan farm needed to raise money, and this was a task which was always there in the background. Even when you had successfully performed every other task, the problem of money always remained, a persistent, nagging worry at the back of one's mind. Mma Potokwane prided herself on her competence in this. If something was needed—a new set of pots for one of the houses, or a pair of shoes for a child whose shoes were wearing thin—she would find a donor who could be persuaded to come up with the money. Few people could resist Mma Potokwane, and there had been an occasion when the Vice-President of Botswana himself, a generous man who prided himself on his open door policy, had thought ruefully of those countries where it was inconceivable that any citizen could claim the right to see the second most important person in the country. Mma Potokwane had made him promise to find somebody to sell her building materials, and he had agreed before he had thought much about it. The building materials had been purchased from a firm which was prepared to sell them cheaply, but it had taken up a great deal of time.

At the very head of Mma Potokwane's list of supporters was Mr J.L.B. Matekoni. She had relied on him for years to take care of various bits of machinery on the orphan farm, including the water pump, which he had now insisted on being replaced, and the minivan in which the orphans were driven into town. This was an old vehicle, exhausted by years of bumping along on the dusty road to the orphanage, and had it not been for Mr J.L.B. Matekoni's expert hand, it would have long since come to the end of its life. But it was a van which he understood, and it was blessed with a Bedford engine that had been built to last and last, like a strong old mule that pulls a cart. The orphan farm could probably afford a new van, but Mma Potokwane saw no reason to spend money on something new when you had something old which was still working.

That Saturday morning, as they sorted out the carpet pieces for the sale, Mma Potokwane suddenly looked at her watch and saw that it was almost time for Mr J.L.B. Matekoni to arrive. She had asked him whether he could come out to look at a ladder which was broken and needed welding. A new ladder would not have cost a great deal, and would probably have been safer, but why buy a new ladder, Mma Potokwane had asked herself. A new ladder might be shiny, but would hardly have the strength of their old metal ladder, which had belonged to the railways and had been given to them almost ten years ago.

She left the housemothers discussing a round piece of green carpet and returned to her office. She had baked a cake for Mr J.L.B. Matekoni, as she usually did, but this time she had taken particular care to make it sweet and rich. She knew that Mr J.L.B. Matekoni liked fruit cake, and particularly liked raisins, and she had thrown several extra handfuls of these into the mixture, just for him. The broken ladder might have been the ostensible reason for his invitation, but she had other business in mind and there was nothing better than a cake to facilitate agreement.

When Mr J.L.B. Matekoni eventually did arrive, she was ready for him, sitting directly in front of the fan in her office, feeling the benefit of the blast of air from the revolving blades, looking out of the window at the lushness of the trees outside. Although Botswana was a dry country, at the end of the rainy season it was always green, and there were pockets of shade at every turn. It was only at the beginning of the summer, before the rains arrived, that everything was desiccated and brown. That was when the cattle became thin, sometimes painfully so, and it broke the heart of a cattle-owning people to see the herds nibbling at the few dry shreds of grass that remained, their heads lowered in lassitude and in weakness. And it would be like that until the purple clouds stacked up to the east and the wind brought the smell of rain—rain which would fall in silver sheets over the land.

That, of course, was if the rain came. Sometimes there were droughts, and a whole season would go by with very little rainfall, and the dryness would become an ache, always there, like dust in the throat. Botswana was lucky of course; she could import grain, but there were countries which could not, for they had no money, and in those places there was nothing to stand between the people and starvation. That was Africa's burden, and by and large it was borne with dignity; but it still caused pain to Mma Potokwane to know that her fellow Africans faced such suffering.

Now, though, the trees were covered with green leaves, and it was easy for Mr J.L.B. Matekoni to find a shady place for his car outside the orphan farm offices. As he emerged from the car, a small boy came up to him and took his hand. The child looked up at him with grave eyes, and Mr J.L.B. Matekoni smiled down on him. Reaching into his pocket, he withdrew a handful of wrapped peppermints, and slipped these into the palm of the child's hand.

"I saw you there, Mr J.L.B. Matekoni," said Mma Potokwane, as her visitor entered her room. "I saw you give sweets to that child. That child is cunning. He knows you are a kind man."

"I am not a kind man," said Mr J.L.B. Matekoni. "I am an ordinary mechanic."

Mma Potokwane laughed. "You are not an ordinary mechanic. You are the best mechanic in Botswana! Everybody knows that."

"No," said Mr J.L.B. Matekoni. "Only you think that."

Mma Potokwane shook her head vigorously. "Then why does the British High Commissioner take his car to you? There are many big garages in Botswana who would like to service a car like that. But he still goes to you. Always."

"I cannot say why," said Mr J.L.B. Matekoni. "But I think that he is a good man and likes to go to a small garage." He was too modest to accept her praise, and yet he was aware of his reputation. Of course, if people knew about his apprentices, and how bad they were, they might think differently of Tlokweng Road Speedy Motors, but the apprentices were not going to be there forever. In fact, they were due to complete their training in a couple of months and that would be the end of them. How peaceful it would be once they had moved on! How comfortable it would be not to have to think of the damage that they were doing to the cars entrusted to him. It would be a new freedom for him; a release from a worry which hung about his shoulders each day. He had done his best to train them properly, and they had picked up something over the years, but they were impatient, and that was a fatal flaw in the personality of any mechanic. Donkeys and cars required patience.

One of the older girls had made tea, and now she brought this in, together with the rich fruit cake on a plate. Mr J.L.B. Matekoni saw the cake, and for a moment he frowned. He knew Mma Potokwane, and the presence of a large cake, specially made for the occasion, was an unambiguous signal that she had a request to make of him. A cake of this size, and emitting such a strong smell of raisins, would mean a major mechanical problem. The minivan? He had replaced the brake pads recently, but he was concerned about the engine seals. At that age, engine seals could go and the block could heat up and . . .

"I've made you a cake," said Mma Potokwane brightly.

"You are a very generous person, Mma," said Mr J.L.B. Matekoni flatly. "You always remember that I like raisins."

"I have many more packets of raisins," said Mma Potokwane, making a generous gesture, as might one with an unlimited supply of raisins. She reached over to the plate and cut a large portion of cake for her guest. Mr J.L.B. Matekoni watched her, and he thought: once I eat this cake I will have to say yes. But then he went on to think: I always say yes anyway, cake or no cake. What difference is there?

"I should think that Mma Ramotswe makes you many cakes these days," said Mma Potokwane as she slid a generous portion of cake onto her own plate. "She is a good cook, I think."

Mr J.L.B. Matekoni nodded. "She is best at cooking pumpkin and things like that," he said. "But she can also make cakes. You ladies are very clever."

"Yes," agreed Mma Potokwane, pouring the tea. "We are much cleverer than you men, but unfortunately you do not know that."

Mr J.L.B. Matekoni looked at his shoes. It was probably true, he thought. It was difficult being a man sometimes, particularly when women reminded one of the fact that one was a man. But there were clever men about, he thought, and these men would give ladies like Mma Potokwane a good run for their money. The problem was that he was not one of these clever men.

Mr J.L.B. Matekoni looked out of the window. He thought that perhaps he should say something, but nothing came into his mind. Outside the window, the branch of the flamboyant tree, on which a few red flowers still grew, moved almost imperceptibly. New seed pods were growing, while last year's pods, long blackened strips, clung to branches here and there. They were good trees, flamboyants, he thought, with their shade and their red flowers, and their delicate fronds of tiny leaves, like feathers, swaying gently in the wind . . . He stopped. The thin green branch just outside the open window seemed to be unwinding itself and extending tentatively, as if some exaggerated process of growth were occurring.

He rose to his feet, putting down his half-finished piece of cake.

"You've seen something?" asked Mma Potokwane. "Are the children up to something out there?"

Mr J.L.B. Matekoni took a step closer to the window and then stopped. "There is a snake on that branch out there, Mma. A green snake."

Mma Potokwane gasped and stood up to peer out of her window. She narrowed her eyes briefly, peering into the foliage, and then reached suddenly for Mr J.L.B. Matekoni's arm.

"You are right, Rra! There is a snake! Ow! Look at it!"

"Yes," said Mr J.L.B. Matekoni. "It's a long snake too. Look, its tail goes all the way down there."

"You must kill it, Rra," said Mma Potokwane. "I will fetch you a stick."

Mr J.L.B. Matekoni nodded. He knew that people were always telling you not to kill snakes on sight, but you could not allow snakes to come so close to all the orphans. It might be different in the bush, where there was a place for snakes, and they had their own roads and paths, going this way and that, but here it was different. This was the orphan farm front yard, and at any moment the snake could drop down on an orphan as he or she walked under that tree. Mma Potokwane was right; he would have to kill the snake.

Armed with the broomstick which Mma Potokwane had fetched from a cupboard, Mr J.L.B. Matekoni, followed at a discreet distance by the matron, walked round the corner of the office building. The syringa tree seemed higher when viewed from outside, and he wondered whether he would be able to reach the branch on which the snake had been sitting. If he could not, then there was nothing that he could do. They would simply have to warn the orphans to stay away from that tree for the time being.

"Just climb up there and hit it," whispered Mma Potokwane. "Look! There it is. It is not moving now."

"I cannot go up there," protested Mr J.L.B. Matekoni. "If I get too close, it could bite me." He shuddered as he spoke. These green tree snakes, boomslangs they called them, were amongst the most poisonous snakes, worse even than the mambas, some people said, because they had no serum in Botswana to deal with their bite. They had to telephone through to South Africa to get supplies of it if somebody was bitten.

"But you must climb up," urged Mma Potokwane. "Otherwise, it will get away."

Mr J.L.B. Matekoni looked at her, as if to confirm the order. He looked for some sign that she did not really mean this, but there was none. He could not climb up the tree, into the snake's domain; he simply could not.

"I cannot," he said. "I cannot climb up there. I shall try to reach him with my stick from here. I shall poke at the branch."

Mma Potokwane looked doubtful, standing back as he took a tentative step forward. She raised a hand to watch as the broom handle moved up into the foliage of the tree. For his part Mr J.L.B. Matekoni held his breath; he was not a cowardly man, and indeed was braver than most. He never shirked his duty and knew that he had to deal with this snake, but the way to deal with snakes was to keep an advantage over them, and while it was in the tree this snake was in its element.

What happened next was the subject of much discussion amongst the staff of the orphan farm and amongst the small knot of orphans which was by now watching from the security of the office verandah. Mr J.L.B. Matekoni might have touched the snake with the broom handle or he might not. It is possible that the snake saw the stick approaching and decided on evasive action, for these are shy snakes, in spite of their powerful venom, and do not seek confrontation. It moved, and moved quickly, slipping through the leaves and branches with a fluid, undulating motion. Within a few seconds it was sliding down the trunk of the tree, impossibly attached, and then was upon the ground and darting, arrow-like, across the baked earth. Mma Potokwane let out a shriek, as the snake seemed to be heading for her, but then it swerved and shot away towards a large hibiscus bush that grew on a patch of grass behind the office. Mr J.L.B. Matekoni gave a shout, and pursued it with his broom, thumping the end of the stick upon the earth. The snake moved faster, and reached the grass, which seemed to help it in its flight. Mr J.L.B. Matekoni stopped; he did not wish to kill this long green stripe of life, which would surely not linger here any longer and was no danger to anyone. He turned to Mma Potokwane, who had raised her hand to her mouth and had uttered a brief ululation, as was traditional, and quite proper, at moments of celebration.

"You brave man!" she shouted. "You chased that snake away!"

"Not really," said Mr J.L.B. Matekoni. "I think it had decided to go anyway."

Mma Potokwane would have none of this. Turning to the group of orphans, who were chattering excitedly amongst themselves, she said, "You see this uncle? You see how he has saved us all from this snake?"

"Ow!" called out one of the orphans. "You are very brave, uncle."

Mr J.L.B. Matekoni looked away in embarrassment. Handing back the broom to Mma Potokwane, he turned to go back into the office, where the rest of his cake was awaiting him. He noticed that his hands were shaking.

"NOW," SAID Mma Potokwane as she placed another, particularly generous, slice of cake on Mr J.L.B. Matekoni's plate. "Now we can talk. Now I know you are a brave man, which I always suspected anyway."

"You must stop calling me that," he said. "I am no braver than any other man."

Mma Potokwane seemed not to hear. "A brave man," she went on. "And I have been looking for a brave man now for over a week. At last I have found him."

Mr J.L.B. Matekoni frowned. "You have had snakes for that long? What about the men around here? What about the husbands of all those housemothers? Where are they?"

"Oh, not snakes," said Mma Potokwane. "We have seen no other snakes. This is about something else. I have a plan which needs a brave man. And you are the obvious person. We need a brave man who is also well-known."

"I am not well-known," said Mr J.L.B. Matekoni quickly.

"But you are! Everybody knows your garage. Everybody has seen you standing outside it, wiping your hands on a cloth. Everybody who drives past says, 'There's Mr J.L.B. Matekoni in front of his garage. That is him.'"

Mr J.L.B. Matekoni looked down at his plate. He felt a strong sense of foreboding, but he would eat the cake nonetheless while Mma Potokwane revealed whatever it was that she had in store for him. He would be strong this time, he thought. He had stood up to her not all that long ago on the question of the pump, and the need to replace it; now he would stand up to her again. He picked up the piece of cake and bit off a large piece. The raisins tasted even better now, in the presence of danger.

"I want you to help me raise money," said Mma Potokwane,"We have a boy who can sing very well. He is sixteen now, one of the older boys, and Mr Slater at the Maitisong Festival wants to send him to Cape Town to take part in a competition. But this costs money, and this boy has none, because he is just an orphan. He can only go if we raise the money for him. It will be a big thing for Botswana if he goes, and a big thing for that boy too."

Mr J.L.B. Matekoni put down the rest of the cake. He need not have worried, he thought: this sounded like a completely reasonable request. He would sell raffle tickets at the garage if she wanted, or donate a free car service as a prize. Why that should require courage, he could not understand.

And then it became clear. Mma Potokwane picked up her tea cup, took a sip of tea, and then announced her plan.

"I'd like you to do a sponsored parachute jump, Mr J.L.B. Matekoni," she said.

CHAPTER THREE

MMA RAMOTSWE VISITS HER COUSIN
IN MOCHUDI, AND THINKS

MMA RAMOTSWE did not see Mr J.L.B. Matekoni that Saturday, as she had driven up to Mochudi in her tiny white van. She planned to stay there until Sunday, leaving the children to be looked after by Mr J.L.B. Matekoni. These were the foster children from the orphan farm, whom Mr J.L.B. Matekoni had agreed to take into his home, without consulting Mma Ramotswe. But she had been unable to hold this against him, even if many women would have felt that they should have been consulted about the introduction of children into their lives; it was typical of his generosity that he should do something like this. After a few days, the children had come to stay with her, which was better than their living in his house, with its engine parts that littered the floor and with its empty store cupboards (Mr J.L.B. Matekoni did not bother to buy much food). And so they had moved to the house in Zebra Drive, the girl and her brother; the girl in a wheelchair, for illness had left her unable to walk, and the brother, much younger than she, and still needing special attention after all that had happened to him.

Mma Ramotswe had no particular reason to go up to Mochudi, but it was the village in which she had grown up and one never really needed an excuse to visit the place in which one had spent one's childhood. That was the marvellous thing about going back to one's roots; there was no need for explanation. In Mochudi everybody knew who she was: the daughter of Obed Ramotswe, who had gone off to Gaborone, where she had made a bad marriage to a trumpet player she had met on a bus. That was all common knowledge, part of the web of memories which made up the village life of Botswana. In that world, nobody needed to be a stranger; everybody could be linked in some way with others, even a visitor; for visitors came for a reason, did they not? They would be associated, then, with the people whom they were visiting. There was a place for everybody.

Mma Ramotswe had been thinking a great deal recently about how people might be fitted in. The world was a large place, and one might have thought that there was enough room for everybody. But it seemed that this was not so. There were many people who were unhappy, and wanted to move. Often they wished to come to the more fortunate countries—such as Botswana—in order to make more of their lives. That was understandable, and yet there were those who did not want them. This is our place, they said; you are not welcome.

It was so easy to think like that. People wanted to protect themselves from those they did not know. Others were different; they talked different languages and wore different clothes. Many people did not want them living close to them, just because of these differences. And yet, they were people, were they not? They thought the same way, and had the same hopes as anybody else did. They were our brothers and sisters, whichever way you looked at it, and you could not turn a brother or sister away.

Mochudi was busy. There was to be a wedding at the Dutch Reformed Church that afternoon, and the relatives of the bride were arriving from Serowe and Mahalapye. There was also some-

thing happening at one of the schools—a sports day, it seemed—
and as she passed the field (or patch of dust, she noted ruefully) a
teacher in a green floppy hat was shouting at a group of children
in running shorts. Ahead of her on the road a couple of donkeys
ambled aimlessly, flicking at the flies with their moth-eaten tails.
It was, in short, a typical Mochudi Saturday.

Mma Ramotswe went to her cousin's house and sat on a stool
in the lelapa, the small, carefully swept yard which forms the
immediate curtilage of the traditional Botswana house. Mma
Ramotswe was always pleased to see her cousin, as these visits
gave her the opportunity to catch up on village news. This was
information one would never see in any newspaper, yet it was every
bit as interesting—more so, in many respects—than the great
events of the world which the newspapers reported. So she sat on a
traditional stool, the seat of which was woven from thin strips of
rough-cured leather, and listened to her cousin tell her what had
taken place. Much had happened since Mma Ramotswe's last
visit. A minor headman, known for his tendency to drink too
much beer, had fallen into a well, but had been saved because a
young boy passing by had happened to mention that he had seen
somebody jump into the well.

"They almost didn't believe that boy," said the cousin. "He
was a boy who was always telling lies. But happily somebody
decided to check."

"That boy will grow up to be a politician," said Mma
Ramotswe. "That will be the best job for him."

The cousin had shrieked with laughter. "Yes, they are very
good at lying. They are always promising us water for every house,
but they never bring it. They say that there are not enough pipes.
Maybe next year."

Mma Ramotswe shook her head. Water was the source of

many problems in a dry country and the politicians did not make it any easier by promising water when they had none to deliver.

"If the opposition would only stop arguing amongst themselves," the cousin went on, "they would win the election and get rid of the government. That would be a good thing, do you not think?"

"No," said Mma Ramotswe.

The cousin stared at her. "But it would be very different if we had a new government," she said.

"Would it?" asked Mma Ramotswe. She was not a cynical woman, but she wondered whether one set of people who looked remarkably like another set of people would run things any differently. But she did not wish to provoke a political argument with her cousin, and so she changed the subject by asking after the doings of a local woman who had killed a neighbour's goat because she thought that the neighbour was flirting with her husband. It was a long-running saga and was providing a great deal of amusement for everyone.

"She crept out at night and cut the goat's throat," said the cousin. "The goat must have thought she was a tokolosh, or something like that. She is a very wicked woman."

"There are many like that," said Mma Ramotswe. "Men think that women can't be wicked, but we are quite capable of being wicked too."

"Even more wicked than men," said the cousin. "Women are much more wicked, don't you agree?"

"No," said Mma Ramotswe. She thought that the levels of male and female wickedness were about the same; it just took slightly different forms.

The cousin looked peevishly at Mma Ramotswe. "Women have not had much of a chance to be wicked in a big way," she muttered. "Men have taken all the best jobs, where you can be truly wicked. If women here were allowed to be generals and presidents and the like, then they would be very wicked, same as all those wicked men. Just give them the chance. Look at how those lady generals have behaved."

Mma Ramotswe picked up a piece of straw and examined it closely. "Name one," she said.

The cousin thought, but no names came to her, at least no names of generals. "There was an Indian lady called Mrs Gandhi."

"And did she shoot people?" asked Mma Ramotswe.

"No," said the cousin. "Somebody shot her. But . . ."

"There you are," said Mma Ramotswe. "I assume that it was a man who shot her, or was it some lady, do you think?"

The cousin said nothing. A small boy was peering over the wall of the lelapa, staring at the two women. His eyes were large and round, and his arms, which protruded from a scruffy red shirt, were thin. The cousin pointed at him.

"He cannot speak, that little boy," she said. "His tongue does not work properly. So he just watches the other children play."

Mma Ramotswe smiled at him, and called out to him gently in Setswana. But the little boy might not have heard, for he turned away without replying and walked slowly away on his skinny legs. Mma Ramotswe was silent for a moment, imagining what it would be like to be a little boy like that, thin and voiceless. I am fortunate, she thought, and turned to say to her cousin, "We are lucky, aren't we? Here we are, traditionally built ladies, and there's that poor little boy with his thin arms and legs. And we can talk and he can make no sound at all."

The cousin nodded. "We are very lucky to be who we are," she said. "We are fortunate ladies, sitting here in the sun with so much to talk about."

So much to talk about—and so little to do. Here in Mochudi, away from the bustle of Gaborone, Mma Ramotswe could feel herself lapsing again into the rhythms of country life, a life much slower and more reflective than life in town. There was still time and space to think in Gaborone, but it was so much easier here, where one might look out up to the hill and watch the thin wisps of cloud, no more than that, float slowly across the sky; or listen to the cattle bells and the chorus of the cicadas. This was what it meant to live in Botswana; when the rest of the world might work itself into a frenzy of activity, one might still sit, in the space before a house with ochre walls, a mug of bush tea in one's hand, and talk about very small things: headmen in wells, goats and jealousy.

CHAPTER FOUR

A WOMAN WHO KNOWS ABOUT HAIR

T HAT MONDAY, Mma Ramotswe had an appointment. Most of her clients did not bother to arrange a time to see her, preferring to drop in unannounced and—in some cases—without disclosing their identity. Mma Ramotswe understood why people should wish to do this. It was not easy to consult a detective agency, especially if one had a problem of a particularly private nature, and many people had to pluck up considerable courage before they knocked on her door. She understood that doctors sometimes encountered similar behaviour; that patients would talk about everything except the real problem and then, at the last moment, mention what was really troubling them. She had read somewhere—in one of the old magazines that Mma Makutsi liked to page through—of a doctor who had been consulted by a man wearing a paper bag over his head. Poor man, thought Mma Ramotswe. It must be terrible to feel so embarrassed about something that one would have to wear a paper bag over one's head! What was wrong with that man? she wondered. Things did go wrong with men sometimes that they were ashamed to talk about, but there was really no need to feel that way.

Mma Ramotswe had never encountered embarrassment of

such a degree, but she had certainly had to draw stories out of people. This happened most commonly with women who had been let down by their husbands, or who suspected that their husbands were having an affair. Such women could feel anger and a sense of betrayal, both of which were entirely understandable, but they could also feel shame that such a thing had happened to them. It was as if it was their fault that their husband had taken up with another woman. This could be so, of course; there were women who drove their husbands away, but in most cases it was because the husband had become bored with his marriage and wanted to see a younger woman. They were always younger, Mma Ramotswe reflected; only rich ladies were able to take up with younger men.

The thought of rich ladies reminded her: the woman who was coming to see her that day was undoubtedly a rich lady. Mma Holonga was well-known in Gaborone as the founder of a chain of hairdressing salons. The salons were successful, but what had proved even more profitable was her invention, and marketing, of Special Girl Hair Braiding Preparation. This was one of those mixtures which women put on their hair before they braided it; its efficacy was doubtful, but the hair products market was not one which required a great deal of scientific evidence. What mattered was that there was a sufficient number of people who believed that their favourite preparation worked.

Mma Ramotswe had never met Mma Holonga. She had seen her picture in *Mmegi* and the *Botswana Guardian* from time to time, and in the photographs she had noticed a pleasant, rather round face. She knew, too, that Mma Holonga lived in a house in the Village, not far from Mr J.L.B. Matekoni. She was intrigued to meet her, because from what she had seen in the newspapers she had formed the impression that Mma Holonga was an unusual rich lady. Many such women were spoilt and demanding, and frequently had an exaggerated idea of their own importance. Mma Holonga did not seem like that.

And when she arrived for her appointment, at exactly the right time (which was another point in her favour), Mma Holonga confirmed Mma Ramotswe's advance impressions.

"You are very kind to see me," she said as she sat down on the chair in front of Mma Ramotswe's desk. "I can imagine how busy you must be."

"Sometimes I am busy," said Mma Ramotswe. "And then sometimes I am not. I am not busy today. I am just sitting here."

"That is very good," said Mma Holonga. "It is good just to sit sometimes. I like to do that, if I get the chance. I just sit."

"There is a lot to be said for that," agreed Mma Ramotswe. "Although we would not want people to do it all the time, would we?"

"Oh no," said Mma Holonga hurriedly. "I would never recommend that."

For a few moments there was silence. Mma Ramotswe looked at the woman in front of her. As the newspaper photographs had suggested, she was traditionally built about the face, but also everywhere else, and her dress was straining at the sides. She should move up a size or two, thought Mma Ramotswe, and then those panels on the side would not look as if they were about to rip. There really was no point in fighting these things: it is far better to admit one's size and indeed there is even a case for buying a slightly larger size. That gives room for manoeuvre.

Mma Holonga was also taking the opportunity to sum up Mma Ramotswe. Comfortable, she thought; not one of these undernourished modern ladies. That is good. But her dress is a bit tight, and she should think of getting a slightly larger size. But she has a friendly face—a good, old-fashioned Botswana face that one can trust, unlike these modern faces which one saw so much of these days.

"I am glad that I came to see you," said Mma Holonga. "I had heard that you were a good person for this sort of thing. That's what people tell me."

Mma Ramotswe smiled. She was a modest person, but a compliment was never unwelcome. And she knew, of course, how important it was to compliment others; not in any insincere way, but to encourage people in their work or to make them feel that their efforts had been worthwhile. She had even complimented the apprentices on one occasion, when they had gone out of their way to help a customer, and for a short time it seemed as if this had inspired them to take a pride in their work. But after a few days she assumed that her words had been forgotten, as they forgot everything else, since they returned to their usual, sloppy habits.

"Oh yes," Mma Holonga continued. "You may not know it, Mma, but your reputation in this town is very high. People say that you are one of the cleverest women in Botswana."

"Oh that cannot be true," said Mma Ramotswe, laughing. "There are many much cleverer ladies in Botswana, ladies with BAs and BScs. There are even lady doctors at the hospital. They must be much cleverer than I am. I have just got my Cambridge Certificate, that is all."

"And I haven't even got that," said Mma Holonga. "But I don't think that I am any less intelligent than those apprentices out there in the garage. I assume they have their Cambridge Certificate too."

"They are a special case," said Mma Ramotswe. "They have passed their Cambridge Certificate, but they are not a very good advertisement for education. Their heads are quite empty. They have nothing in them except thoughts of girls."

Mma Holonga glanced through the doorway to where one of the apprentices could be seen sitting on an upturned oil-drum. She appeared to study him for a moment before she turned back to Mma Ramotswe. Mma Ramotswe noticed; it was only a momentary stare, she thought, but it told her something: Mma Holonga was interested in men. And why should she not be? The days when women had to pretend not to be interested in men were surely over, and now they could talk about it. Mma Ramotswe was not sure whether it was a good idea to talk too openly about men—she had heard some quite shocking things being said by some women, and she would never condone such shamelessness—but it was, on the whole, better for women to be able to express themselves.

"I have come to see you about men," said Mma Holonga suddenly. "That is why I am here."

Mma Ramotswe was taken aback. She had wondered why Mma Holonga had come and had assumed that it was something to do with one of her businesses. But now it seemed it was going to be something rather more personal than that.

"There are many women who come to see me about men," she said quietly. "Men are a major problem for many women."

Mma Holonga smiled at this. "That is no exaggeration, Mma. But many women have problems just with one man. I have problems with four men."

Mma Ramotswe gave a start. This was unexpected: four men! It was conceivable that somebody might have two boyfriends, and hope that neither found out about the other, but to have four! That was an invitation for trouble.

"It's not what you may think," said Mma Holonga hurriedly. "I do not have four boyfriends. At the moment I have no boyfriend, except for these four . . ."

Mma Ramotswe raised her hand. "You should start at the

beginning," she said. "I am getting confused already." She paused. "And to help you talk, I shall make some bush tea. Would you like that?"

Mma Holonga nodded. "I will talk while you are making the tea. Then you will hear all my troubles while the water is boiling."

"I AM a very ordinary lady," Mma Holonga began. "I did not do very well at school, as I have told you. When other girls were looking at their books, I was always looking at magazines. I liked the fashion magazines with all their pictures of bright clothes and smart models. And I specially liked looking at pictures of people's hair and of how hair could be braided and made beautiful with all those beads and henna and things like that.

"I thought it very unfair that God had given African ladies short hair and all the long hair had been taken by everybody else. But then I realised that there was no reason why African hair should not be very beautiful too, although it is not easy to do things with it. I used to braid my friends' hair, and soon I had quite a reputation amongst the other girls at school. They came to see me on Friday afternoons to have their hair braided for the week-end, and I would do it outside our kitchen. The friends would sit on a chair and I would stand behind them, talking and braiding hair in the afternoon sun. I was very happy doing that.

"You'll know all about hair braiding, Mma. You'll know that it can sometimes take a long time. Most of the time I would only spend an hour or two on somebody's hair, but there were times when I spent over two days on a design. I was very proud of all the circles and lines, Mma. I was very proud.

"By the time I was ready to leave school, there was no doubt in my mind what I wanted to do for a living. I had been promised a job in a hair salon that a lady had opened in the African Mall.

She had seen my work and knew that I would bring a lot of business because I was so well-known as a hair braider. She was right. All my friends came to this salon although now they had to pay for me to do their hair.

"After a while I started my own business. I found a small tuck shop that was closing down and I started off in there. It was very cramped, and I had to bring the water I needed in a bucket, but all my customers moved with me and said that they did not mind if the new place was very small. They said that the important thing was to have somebody who really knew about hair, and they said I was such a person. One of them said that a person who knew as much about hair only comes along once or twice in a century. I was very pleased to hear this and asked that person to write out what they had said. I then had a sign-writer paint it on a board and passers-by would stop and read that remark and look at me with respect as I stood there with my scissors ready to cut their hair. I was very happy, Mma. I was very happy.

"I built up my business and eventually I bought a proper salon. Then I bought another one and another after that up in Francistown. Everything went very well and all this time the money was piling up in the bank. I had so much money that I could not really spend it all myself, and so I gave some to my brother and asked him to use it to buy some other businesses for me. He bought me a shop and a place where they make dresses. So I had a factory now, and this made me even richer. I was very happy with all that money, and I went into the bank every Thursday to check how much I had. They were very polite to me now, as I had all that money and banks like people with lots of money.

"But you know what I didn't have, Mma? I didn't have a husband. I had been so busy cutting hair and making money that I had forgotten to get married. Three months ago, when I had my fortieth birthday, I suddenly thought: where is your husband?

Where are all your children? And the answer was that there were none of these. So I decided that I would find a husband. It may be too late to have children now, but at least I would find a husband.

"And do you think that was easy, Mma? What do you think?"

Mma Ramotswe had by now made the bush tea and was pouring it into her client's cup. "I think it would be easy for a lady like you," she said. "I would not think you would find it hard."

"Oh?" said Mma Holonga. "And why would I not find it hard?"

Mma Ramotswe hesitated. She had answered without thinking very much about it, and now she wondered how she would explain herself. She had probably thought that it would be easy for Mma Holonga to find a husband because she was rich. It was easy for rich people to do anything, even to find a husband. But could she say that? Would it not seem insulting to Mma Holonga that the only reason why Mma Ramotswe should think she could find a husband was because she was rich, and not because she was beautiful or desirable.

"There are many men . . ." began Mma Ramotswe, and then stopped. "There are many men looking for wives."

"But many women say that it is not all that easy," said Mma Holonga. "Why should they find it hard while I should find it easy? Can you explain that?"

Mma Ramotswe sighed. It was best to be honest, she thought, and so she said, quite simply, "Money, Mma. That is the reason. You are a lady with a large chain of hair salons. You are a rich lady. There are many men who like rich ladies."

Mma Holonga sat back in her chair and smiled. "Exactly, Mma. I was waiting to see if you would say that. Now I know that you really do understand things."

"But they would also like you because you are an attractive

lady," added Mma Ramotswe hurriedly. "Traditional Botswana men like ladies who are more traditionally shaped. You and I, Mma. We remind men of how things used to be in Botswana before these modern-shaped ladies started to get men all confused."

Mma Holonga nodded, but in a rather distracted fashion. "Yes, Mma. That may be quite true, but I think that my problem remains. I must tell you what happened when I let it be known that I was looking for a suitable husband. A very interesting thing happened." She paused. "But would you pour me more of that tea, Mma? It is very fine tea and I am thirsty again."

"It is bush tea," said Mma Ramotswe as she reached for the tea-pot. "Mma Makutsi—my assistant—and I drink bush tea because it helps us to think."

Mma Holonga raised her refilled cup to her lips and drained it noisily.

"I shall buy bush tea instead of ordinary tea," she said. "I shall put honey in it and drink it every day."

"That would be a very good thing to do," said Mma Ramotswe. "But what about this husband business? What happened?"

Mma Holonga frowned. "It is very difficult for me," she said. "When word got round, then I received many telephone calls. Ten, twenty calls. And they were all from men."

Mma Ramotswe raised an eyebrow. "That is a large number of men," she said.

Mma Holonga nodded. "Of course, I realised that some of them were no good right there and then. One even telephoned from the prison and the telephone was snatched away from him. And one was only a boy, about thirteen or fourteen, I think. But I agreed to see the others, and from these I ended up with a list of four."

"That is a good number to choose from," said Mma Ramotswe. "Not too large a list of men, but not too small."

Mma Holonga seemed pleased by this. She looked at Mma Ramotswe uncertainly. "You do not think it strange to have a list, Mma? Some of my friends . . ."

Mma Ramotswe raised a hand to interrupt her. Many of her clients referred to advice from friends, and in her experience this advice was often wrong. Friends tried to be helpful, but tended to misadvise, largely because they had unrealistic ideas of what the friend whom they were advising was really like. Mma Ramotswe believed that it was usually better to seek the advice of a stranger—not just any stranger, of course, as one could hardly go out onto the street and confide in the first person one encountered, but a stranger whom you knew to be wise. We do not talk about wise men or wise ladies any more, she reflected; their place had been taken, it seemed, by all sorts of shallow people—actors and the like—who were only too ready to pronounce on all sorts of subjects. It was worse, she thought, in other countries, but it was beginning to happen in Botswana and she did not like it. She, for one, would never pay any attention to the views of such people; she would far rather listen to a person who had done something real in life; these people knew what they were talking about.

"I'm not sure if you should worry too much about what your friends think, Mma," she said. "I think that it is a good idea to have a list. What is the difference between a list of things to buy at a shop, or a list of things to do, and a list of men? I do not see the difference."

"I am glad that you think that," said Mma Holonga. "In fact, I have been glad to hear everything that you have said."

Mma Ramotswe was always embarrassed by compliments, and rapidly went on.

"You must tell me about this list," she said. "And you must tell me about what you want me to do."

"I want you to find out about these men," said Mma Holonga. "I want you to see which men are interested in my money and which are interested in me."

Mma Ramotswe clapped her hands in delight. "Oh, this is the sort of work I like," she said. "Judging men! Men are always looking at women and judging them. Now we have the chance to do some judging back. Oh, this is a very good case to take on."

"I can pay you very well," said Mma Holonga, reaching for the large black handbag she had placed by the side of her chair. "If you tell me how much it will cost, I shall pay it."

"I shall send you a bill," said Mma Ramotswe. "That is what we do. Then you can pay me for my time." She paused. "But first, you must tell me about these men, Mma. I shall need some information on them. Then I shall set to work."

Mma Holonga sat back in her seat. "I am happy to talk about men, Mma. And now I shall begin with the first of these men."

Mma Ramotswe looked into her tea cup. It was still half-full of bush tea. That would be enough to see her through one man, perhaps, but not four. So she reached forward, picked up the teapot, and offered to fill Mma Holonga's cup before attending to her own. That was the old Botswana way of doing things, and that is how Mma Ramotswe behaved. Modern people could say what they liked, but nobody had ever come up with a better way of doing things and in Mma Ramotswe's view nobody ever would.

CHAPTER FIVE

MR J.L.B. MATEKONI HAS CAUSE
TO REFLECT

IT WAS some time before it dawned on Mr J.L.B. Matekoni that Mma Potokwane may have thought that he was agreeing to her proposition. His own recollection of what had happened was very clear. He had said, "I shall think about it, Mma," which is very different—as anybody could see—from saying that one would definitely do something. It might have been better had he refused her there and then, but Mr J.L.B. Matekoni was a kind man and like all kind men he did not enjoy saying no. There were many who had no such compunction, of course; they would refuse things outright, even if it meant hurting another's feelings.

Mr J.L.B. Matekoni thought very carefully. After the initial bombshell, when Mma Potokwane had revealed what she had in mind, he had remained silent for a moment. At first, he thought that he had misheard her, and that she had said that she wanted him to *fix* a parachute, just as she was always asking him to fix some piece of equipment. But of course she had not asked him that, as there would have been plenty of people around the orphan farm who would be much better placed to fix a parachute than he. Fixing a parachute was a sewing job, he assumed, and most of the housemothers were adept at that; they were always sewing the orphans' clothes, repairing rents in the seats of boys' trousers or undoing the hems of skirts that were now a little bit too short. These ladies could easily have stitched up a torn parachute, even if the parachute would end up with a patch made out of a boy's trousers. No, that was not what Mma Potokwane could have had in mind.

Her next remark made this clear. "It's a very good way of raising money," she had said. "The hardship project did it last year. That man from the radio—the well-known one with the funny voice—he agreed to jump. And then that girl who almost became Miss Botswana said she would jump too. They raised a lot of money. A lot."

"But I cannot jump," Mr J.L.B. Matekoni had protested. "I have never even been in an aeroplane. I would not like to jump from one."

It was as if Mma Potokwane had not heard him. "It is a very easy thing to do. I have spoken to somebody in the Flying Club and they say that they can teach you how to do it. They have a book, too, which shows you how to put your feet when you land. It is very simple. Even I could do it."

"Then why don't you?" he had said, but not loudly enough to be heard, for Mma Potokwane had continued as if he had not spoken.

"There is no reason to be afraid," she said. "I think that it will be very comfortable riding down in the air like that. They might drop you over one of our fields and I will get one of the housemothers to have a cake ready for you when you land. And we have a stretcher too. We can have that close by, just in case."

"I do not want to do it," Mr J.L.B. Matekoni had intended to say, but for some reason the words came out as, "I'll think about it."

And that, he realised, was where he had made his mistake. Of course it would be easy enough to undo. All that he would have to do would be to telephone Mma Potokwane and tell her, as unambiguously and as finally as he could, that he had now thought about it and he had decided that he would not do it. He would be happy to give some money to whomsoever she managed to persuade to do it for her, but that person, he was sorry to say, would not be him. This was the only way with Mma Potokwane. One had to be firm with her, just as he had been firm with her on the issue of the pump. One had to stand up to a woman like that.

The difficulty, of course, with standing up to women was that it appeared to make little difference. At the end of the day, a man was no match for a woman, especially if that woman was some-body like Mma Potokwane. The only thing to do was to try to avoid situations where women might corner you. And that was difficult, because women had a way of ensuring that you were neatly boxed in, which was exactly what had happened to him. He should have been more careful. He should have been on his guard when she offered him cake. That was her technique, he now understood; just as Eve had used an apple to trap Adam, so Mma Potokwane used fruit cake. Fruit cake, apples; it made no difference really. Oh foolish, weak men!

Mr J.L.B. Matekoni looked at his watch. It was nine o'clock in the morning, and he should have been at the garage by eight, at the latest. The apprentices had plenty to do—simple servicing tasks that morning—and he could probably leave them to get on with it, but he did not like to leave the business in their hands for too long. He looked out of the window. It was a comfortable sort of day, not too hot for the time of year, and it would be good to drive out into the lands somewhere and just walk along a path. But he could not do that, as he had his clients to think of. The best thing to do was to stop thinking about it, and to get on with the ordinary business of the day. There were exhaust pipes to be looked at, tyres to be changed, brake linings to be renewed; these were the things that really mattered, not some ridiculous parachute drop which Mma Potokwane had dreamed up and which he was not proposing to do anyway. That could be disposed of—with a little resolve. All he had to do was to lift up the telephone and say no to Mma Potokwane. He imagined the conversation.

"No, Mma. That's all: no."

"No what?"

"No. I'm not doing it."

"What do you mean no?"

"By no, I mean no. That's what I mean. No."

"No? Oh."

That, at least, was the theory. When it came actually to speaking, it might be considerably more difficult than that. But at least he had an idea of what he might say and the tone he would adopt.

MR J.L.B. MATEKONI, trying—and largely succeeding—not to think of parachutes or aeroplanes, or even the sky, started the short journey from his house to Tlokweng Road Speedy Motors. It was a journey that he had made so often that he knew every bump in the road, every gateway past which he drove, and, extraordinarily, the people whom he would often see standing at much the same place as they always stood. People like their places, Mr J.L.B. Matekoni reflected. There was that rather ragged man who used to walk about the end of Maratadiba Road, looking as if he had lost something. He was the father, he believed, of the maid who worked in one of the houses there and she had given him the spare room in her quarters. That was the right thing for a daughter to do, of course, but if Mr J.L.B. Matekoni were that man, or the daughter for that matter, he would think that the best place for a father who was slightly confused would be back in the village, or even out at the lands or at a cattle post. In the village he would be able to stand in one spot and watch everything happen without his moving about. He could watch cattle, which was very important for older people, and a good hobby for older men. There was a great deal to be learned just by watching cattle and noting their different colours. That would have kept that man busy.

And then, just round the corner, on Boteli Road, on Fridays and Saturdays one might see a very interesting car parked under the shade of a thorn tree. The car belonged to the brother of a man who lived in one of the houses on Boteli Road. He was a butcher from Lobatse, who came up to Gaborone for the weekends, which started, for him, on Friday morning. Mr J.L.B. Matekoni had seen his butchery store down in Lobatse. It was large and modern, with a picture of a cow painted on the side. In addition, this man owned a plastering business, and so Mr J.L.B. Matekoni imagined that he was a fairly wealthy man, at least by the standards of Lobatse, if not the standards of Gaborone. But it was not his prosperity which singled him out in the eyes of Mr J.L.B. Matekoni; it was the fact that he had such a fine car and had clearly taken such good care of it.

This car was a Rover 90, made in 1955, and therefore very old. It was painted blue, and on the front there was a silver badge showing a boat with a high prow. The first time he had driven past it, Mr J.L.B. Matekoni had stopped to examine it and had noted the fine red leather seats and the gleaming silver of the gear lever. These external matters had not impressed him; it was the knowledge of what lay within: the knowledge of the 2.6-litre engine with its manual transmission *and its famous free wheel option*. That was something one would not see these days, and indeed Mr J.L.B. Matekoni had once brought his apprentices to look at the car, from the outside, so that they could get some sense of fine engineering. He knew of course that there was very little chance of that, but he tried anyway. The apprentices had whistled, and the older one, Charlie, had said, "That is a very fine car, Rra! Ow!" But no sooner had Mr J.L.B. Matekoni turned his back for a moment than that very same apprentice had leant forward to admire himself in the car's wing mirror.

Mr J.L.B. Matekoni had realised then that it was hopeless. Between these young men and himself there was a gulf that simply could not be crossed. The apprentice had recognised that it was a fine car, but had he really understood what it was that made it fine? He doubted that. They were impressed with the spoilers and flashy aluminium wheels that car manufacturers added these days; things which meant nothing, just nothing, to a real mechanic like Mr J.L.B. Matekoni. These were the externals, the outside trim designed, as often as not, to impress those who had no knowledge of cars. For the real mechanic, mechanical beauty lay in the accuracy and intricacy of the thousand moving pieces within the breast of the car: the rods, the cogs, the pistons. These were the things that mattered, not the inanimate parts that did nothing but reflect the sun.

Mr J.L.B. Matekoni slowed down and gazed at the fine car under the thorn tree. As he did so, he noticed, to his alarm, that there was something under the car—something that a casual observer might not notice but which he would never miss. Drawing up at the side of the road, he switched off the engine of his truck and got out of the cab. Then, walking over to the blue Rover, he went down on his hands and knees and peered at the dark underbelly of the car. Yes, it was as he thought; and now he went down on his stomach and crawled under the car to get a better view. It took him only a moment to realise what was wrong, of course, but the sight made him draw in his breath sharply. A pool of oil had leaked out onto the ground below the car and had stained the sand black.

"What are you doing, Rra?"

The sound surprised Mr J.L.B. Matekoni, but he knew better than to lift his head up sharply; that was the sort of thing that the apprentices kept doing. They often bumped their heads on the bottom of cars when the telephone rang or when something else disturbed them. It was a normal human reaction to look up when disturbed, but a mechanic learned quickly to control it. Or a mechanic should learn that quickly; the apprentices had not done so, and he suspected that they never would. Mma Makutsi knew this, of course, and she had once rather mischievously called out Charlie's name when he was underneath a car. "Charlie," she had cried, and there had followed a dull thump as the unfortunate young man had sat up and hit his head on the sump of the car. Mr J.L.B. Matekoni had not really approved of this little joke, but he had found it difficult not to smile when he caught her eye. "I was just checking up that you were all right," shouted Mma Makutsi. "Be careful of your head down there. That brain needs to be looked after, you know."

Mr J.L.B. Matekoni wriggled his way out from under the car and stood up, dusting his trousers as he did so. As he had thought, it was the butcher himself, a corpulent man with a thick neck, like the neck of a bull. It was obvious to anyone, from the very first glance, that this was a wealthy man, even if they did not know about the butchery and the plastering business, nor indeed about this wonderful car with its silver badge.

"I was looking at your car, Rra," he said. "I was underneath it."

"So I see," said the butcher. "I saw your legs sticking out. When I saw that, I knew that there was somebody under my car."

Mr J.L.B. Matekoni smiled. "You must be wondering what I was doing, Rra."

The butcher nodded. "You are right. That is what I was wondering."

"You see, I am a mechanic," said Mr J.L.B. Matekoni. "I have always thought very highly of this car. It is a very good car."

The butcher seemed to relax. "Oh, I see, Rra. You are one who understands old cars like this. I am happy for you to go back under and look."

Mr J.L.B. Matekoni acknowledged the generosity of the offer. He would go back under the car, but it would be more than out of mere curiosity. If he went back, it would be on a mission of repair. He would have to tell the butcher of what he had seen.

"There is oil, Rra," he began. "Your car is leaking oil."

The butcher lifted up a hand in a gesture of tiredness. There was always oil. It was a risk with old cars. Oil; the smell of burning rubber; mysterious rattles: old cars were like the bush at night—there were always strange sounds and smells. He kept taking the car back to the garage and getting them to fix this problem and that problem, and yet these problems always recurred. And now here was another mechanic—one he did not even know—who was talking about oil leaks.

"I have had trouble with oil," he said. "There are always oil leaks and I always have to put more oil in the front. Every time I make the journey up from Lobatse, I have to put in more oil."

Mr J.L.B. Matekoni grimaced. "That is bad, Rra. But you should not have to do it. If the person who serviced this car made sure that the rubber seal on the rod that holds the oil cylinder was in its proper place, then this sort of thing would not happen." He paused. "I could fix this for you. I could do it in ten minutes."

The butcher looked at him. "I cannot bring the car in to your garage now," he said. "I have to talk to my brother about our sister's boy. He is a difficult boy, that one, and we have to work something out. And anyway, I cannot be paying all sorts of mechanics to look at this car. I have already paid a lot of money to the garage."

Mr J.L.B. Matekoni looked down at his shoes. "I would not have charged you, Rra. That is not why I offered."

For a few moments there was silence. The butcher looked at Mr J.L.B. Matekoni and knew, immediately, what sort of man he was dealing with. And he knew, too, that his assumption that Mr J.L.B. Matekoni would want payment was a gross misreading of the situation; for there were people in Botswana who still believed in the old Botswana ways and who were prepared to do things for others just to help them and not in prospect of some reward. This man, whom he had found lying underneath his car, was such a man. And yet he had paid such a great deal of money to those mechanics and they had assured him that all was in order. And the car, after all, worked reasonably well, even if there was a small problem with oil.

The butcher frowned, slipping a hand inside his collar and tugging at it, as if to loosen the material. "I do not think there can be anything wrong with my car," he said. "I think that you must be wrong, Rra."

Mr J.L.B. Matekoni shook his head. Without saying any-thing, he pointed to the edge of the dark oil stain, just discernible beneath the body of the car. The butcher's gaze followed his hand, and he shook his head vigorously. "It is impossible," he said. "I take this car to a good garage. I pay a great deal of money to have it looked after. They are always tinkering with the engine."

Mr J.L.B. Matekoni raised an eyebrow. "Always tinkering? Who are these people?" he asked.

The butcher gave the name of the garage, and Mr J.L.B. Matekoni knew immediately. He had spent years trying to improve the image of the motor trade, but whatever he, and oth-ers like him, did they would always be thwarted by the activities of people like the butcher's mechanics; if indeed they were mechanics at all—Mr J.L.B. Matekoni had strong doubts about the qualifications of some of them.

Mr J.L.B. Matekoni took his handkerchief out of his pocket and wiped his brow.

'If you would let me look at the engine, Rra," he said. "I could very quickly check your oil level. Then we would know whether it was safe for you to drive off to have more oil put in."

The butcher hesitated for a moment. There was something humiliating about being called to account in this way, and yet it would be churlish to reject an offer of help. This man was obviously sincere, and seemed to know what he was talking about; so he reached into his pocket for the car keys, opened the driver's door, and set about pulling the silver-topped lever that would release the catch on the engine cover.

Mr J.L.B. Matekoni stood back respectfully. The revealing of an engine of this nature—an engine which was older than the Republic of Botswana itself—was a special moment, and he did not want to show unseemly curiosity as the beautiful piece of engineering was exposed to view. So he stood where he was and only leaned forward slightly once he could see the engine; and quickly drew in his breath, and was silent—not in admiration, as he had expected, but in shock. For this was not the engine of a 1955 Rover 90, lovingly preserved; he saw, instead, an engine which had been cobbled together with all manner of parts. A flimsy carburettor, of recent vintage and crude construction; a modern oil filter, adapted and tacked onto the only original part that he could make out—the great, solid engine block that had been put into the car at its birth all those years ago. That at least was intact, but what mechanical company it had been obliged to keep!

The butcher looked at him expectantly. "Well, Rra?"

Mr J.L.B. Matekoni found it hard to reply. There were times

when, as a mechanic, one had to give bad news. It was never easy, and one often wished that there were some way round the brute truth. But there were occasions when just nothing could be done, and he feared that this was one of them. "I'm sorry, Rra," he began. "This is very sad. A terrible thing has been done to this car. The engine parts . . ." He could not go on. What had been done was an act of such mechanical vandalism that Mr J.L.B. Matekoni could not find the words to express the feelings within him. So he turned away and shook his head, as might one who had seen some great work of art destroyed before his eyes, cast low by the basest Philistines.

CHAPTER SIX

MR MOPEDI BOBOLOGO

MMA HOLONGA sat back in her chair and closed her eyes. From the other side of the desk, Mma Ramotswe watched her client. She had observed that some people found it easier to tell a story if they shut their eyes, or if they looked down, or focused on something in the distance—something that was there but not there. It did not matter to her; the important thing was that clients should feel comfortable and that they should be able to talk without embarrassment. It might not be easy for Mma Holonga to talk about this, as these were intimate matters of the heart, and if closing her eyes would help, then Mma Ramotswe thought that a good idea. One of her clients, ashamed of what he had to say, had talked from behind cupped hands; that had been difficult, as what he had said had been far from clear. At least Mma Holonga, addressing her from her private darkness, could be understood perfectly well.

"I'll start with the man I like best," she said. "Or at least I think he is the one I like the best."

Then why not marry him? thought Mma Ramotswe. If you liked a man, then surely you could trust your judgment? But no, there were men who were likeable—charming in fact—but who were dangerous to women: Note Makoti, thought Mma Ramotswe. Her own first husband, Note Makoti, was immensely attractive to women, and only later would they discover what sort of man he really was. So Mma Holonga was right: the man you liked might not be the right man.

"Tell me about this man," said Mma Ramotswe. "What does he do?"

Mma Holonga smiled. "He is a teacher."

Mma Ramotswe noted this information on a piece of paper. *First man,* she wrote. *Teacher.* It was important information, because everybody in Botswana had their place, and one simple word could describe a world. Teachers were respected in Botswana, even if so many attitudes were changing. In the past, of course, it had been an even more important thing to be a schoolteacher, and the moral authority of the teacher was recognised by all. Today, more people had studied for diplomas and certificates and these people considered themselves to be every bit as good as teachers. But often they were not, because teachers had wisdom, while many of these people with paper qualifications had not. The wisest man Mma Ramotswe had ever known—her own father, Obed Ramotswe, had no Cambridge Certificate, not even his Standard Six, but that had made no difference. He had wisdom, and that counted for very much more.

She looked out of the window while Mma Holonga began to explain who the teacher was. She tried to concentrate, but the thought of her father had taken her back to Mochudi, and to the memories that the village had for her; of afternoons in the hot season when nothing happened but the heat and when it seemed that nothing could ever have happened; when there was time to sit in front of one's house in the evening and watch the birds flying back to the trees and the sky to the West fill with swathes of red as the sun went down over the Kalahari; when it seemed that you would be fifteen years old for ever and would always be here in Mochudi. And you were not to know then what the world would bring; that the life you imagined for yourself elsewhere might not be as good as the life you already had. Not that this was the case with Mma Ramotswe's life, which had on the whole been a happy one; but for many it was true—those quiet days in their village would prove to be the best time for them.

Mma Ramotswe's thoughts were interrupted by Mma Holonga. "A teacher, Mma," the other woman said. "I said that he was a teacher."

"I'm sorry," said Mma Ramotswe. "I was dreaming there for a moment. A teacher. Yes, Mma, that is a good job to have, in spite of the cheekiness of young people these days. It is still a good thing to be a teacher."

Mma Holonga nodded, acknowledging the truth of this observation. "His name is Bobologo," she went on. "Mopedi Bobologo. He is a teacher at the school over there near the University gate. You know that one."

"I have driven past it many times," said Mma Ramotswe. "And Mr J.L.B. Matekoni, who is the man who runs this garage behind us; he has a house nearby and he says that he can hear the children singing sometimes if the wind is coming from that school."

Mma Holonga listened to this, but was not interested. She did not know Mr J.L.B. Matekoni, and could not picture him, as Mma Ramotswe now did, standing on his verandah, listening to the singing of the children.

"This man is called Mr Mopedi Bobologo, although he is not like the famous Bobologo. This one is tall and thin, because he comes from the North, and they are often tall up there. Like the trees. They are just like the trees up in the North.

"He is a very clever man, this Bobologo. He knows everything about everything. He has read many books, and can tell you what is in all of them. This books says that. This book says this. He knows the contents of many books."

"Oh," said Mma Ramotswe. "There are many, many books. And all the time, more books are coming. It is difficult to read them all."

"It is impossible to read them all," said Mma Holonga. "Even those very clever people at the University of Botswana—people like Professor Tlou—they have not read everything."

"It must be sad for them," observed Mma Ramotswe reflectively. "If it is your job to read books and you can never get to the end of them. You think that you have read all the books and suddenly you see that there are some new ones that have arrived. Then what do you do? You have to start over again."

Mma Holonga shrugged. "I don't know what you do. It is the same with every job, I suppose. Look at hairdressing. You braid one head of hair and then another head of unbraided hair comes along. And so it goes on. You cannot finish your work." She paused. "Even you, Mma. Look at you. You deal with one case and then somebody knocks at the door and there is another case. Your work is never finished."

They were both silent for a moment, thinking of the endless nature of work. It was true, thought Mma Ramotswe, but it was not something to worry too much about. If it were not true, one might have real cause to be concerned.

"Tell me more about this Mr Bobologo," said Mma Ramotswe. "Is he a kind man?"

Mma Holonga thought for a moment. "He is kind, I think. I have seen him smiling at the schoolchildren and he has never spoken roughly to me. I think he is kind."

"Then why has he not been married?" asked Mma Ramotswe. "Or is his wife late?"

"There was a wife," said Mma Holonga. "But she died. He did not have time to get married again, as he was so busy reading. Now he thinks that it is time."

Mma Ramotswe looked out of the window. There was something wrong with this Mr Bobologo; she could sense it. So she wrote on her piece of paper: *No wife. Reads books. Tall and thin.* She looked up. It would not take long to deal with Mr Bobologo, she thought; then they could move on to the second, third, and fourth man. There would be something to worry about with each of them, she thought pessimistically, but then she corrected herself, reminding herself that it was no use giving up on a case before one even started. Clovis Andersen, author of *The Principles of Private Detection*, would never have countenanced that. *Be confident*, he wrote—and Mma Ramotswe remembered the very passage—*Everything can be found out in time. There are very few circumstances in which the true facts are waiting to be tripped over. And never, ever reach a decision before you start.*

That was very wise advice, and Mma Ramotswe was determined to follow it. So while Mma Holonga continued to talk about Mr Bobologo, she deliberately thought of the positive aspects of this man who was being described to her. And there were many. He was very neat, she heard, and he did not drink too much. On one occasion, when they had a meal together, he had made sure that she had the bigger piece of meat and he had taken the smaller. That was a very good sign, was it not? A man who did that must have very fine qualities. And of course he was educated, which would mean that he could teach Mma Holonga things, and improve her outlook on life. All of this was positive, and yet there was still something wrong, and she could not drive the suspicion from her mind. Mr Bobologo would have an ulterior motive. Money? That was the obvious one, but was there something more to it than that?

*   *   *

MMA HOLONGA had just finished talking that morning when Mr J.L.B. Matekoni arrived at the garage. He was preoccupied with his encounter with the butcher and he was eager to tell Mma Ramotswe about it. He had heard a great deal about that other garage, and from time to time he had seen the results of their fumbling when one of their disgruntled clients had switched to Tlokweng Road Speedy Motors. But those cases were but as nothing compared with the deliberate fraud—and there really was no other word for it—which his glance at the engine of the Rover 90 had revealed. This was dishonesty of a calculated and prolonged variety, all perpetrated against a man who had trusted them, and, what was perhaps even more shocking, against an important car that had been placed in their hands. That was a particular and aggravated wrong: a mechanic had a duty towards machinery, and these ones had demonstrably failed to discharge that duty. If you were a conscientious mechanic you would never deliberately subject an engine to stress. Engines had their dignity—yes, that was the word—and Mr J.L.B. Matekoni, as one of Botswana's finest mechanics, was not ashamed to use such terms. It was a question of morality. That was what it was.

As he parked his truck in its accustomed place—under the acacia tree at the side of the garage—Mr J.L.B. Matekoni reflected on the sheer effrontery of those people. He imagined the butcher going into the garage and describing some problem, and being reassured, when he collected the car, that it had been attended to. Perhaps they even lied about the difficulties of obtaining parts; he was sure that they would have charged him for the genuine spare parts, which they would have had to order from a special dealer in South Africa, or even England, all that way away. He thought of the factory in England where they made

Rover cars; under a grey sky, with rain, which they had in such abundance and of which Botswana had so little; and he thought too of those Englishmen, his brother mechanics, standing over the metal lathes and drills that would produce those beautiful pieces of machinery. What would they have felt, he wondered, if they were to know that far away in Botswana there were unscrupulous mechanics prepared to put all sorts of unsuitable parts into the engine which they had so lovingly created? What would they think of Botswana if they knew that? It made him burn with indignation just to contemplate. And he was sure that Mma Ramotswe would share his outrage when he told her. He had noticed her reaction to wrongdoing when she heard about it. She would go quiet, and shake her head, and then she would utter some remark which always expressed exactly what he was feeling, but in a way which he could never achieve. He was a man of machinery, of nuts and bolts and engine blocks, not a man of words. But he appreciated the right words when he heard them, and particularly when they came from Mma Ramotswe, who, in his mind, spoke for Botswana.

Rather than enter the garage through the workshop, Mr J.L.B. Matekoni went round to the side, to the door of the No. 1 Ladies' Detective Agency. Normally this was kept open, which meant that chickens sometimes wandered in and annoyed Mma Makutsi by pecking at the floor around her toes, but today it was closed, which suggested that Mma Ramotswe and Mma Makutsi were out, or that there was a client inside. Mr J.L.B. Matekoni leaned forward to listen at the keyhole, to see if he could hear voices within, and at that moment, as he bent forward, the door was suddenly opened from inside.

Mma Holonga stared in astonishment at the sight of Mr J.L.B. Matekoni, bent almost double. She half turned to Mma

Ramotswe. "There is a man here," she said. "There is a man here listening."

Mma Ramotswe shot Mr J.L.B. Matekoni a warning glance. "He has hurt his back, I think, Mma. That is why he is standing like that. And anyway, it's only Mr J.L.B. Matekoni, who owns the garage. He is entitled to be standing there. He is quite harmless."

Mma Holonga looked again at Mr J.L.B. Matekoni, who, feeling that he had to authenticate Mma Ramotswe's explanation, put a hand to his back and tried to look uncomfortable.

"I thought that he was trying to listen to us," said Mma Holonga. "That's what I thought, Mma."

"No, he would not do that," said Mma Ramotswe. "Sometimes men just stand around. I think that is what he was doing."

"I see," said Mma Holonga, making her way past Mr J.L.B. Matekoni with a sideways glance. "I shall go now, Mma. But I shall wait to hear from you."

"Well, well!" said Mma Ramotswe as they watched Mma Holonga get into her car. "That was very awkward. What were you doing listening in at the keyhole?"

Mr J.L.B. Matekoni laughed. "I was not listening. Or I was not listening, but just trying to hear . . ." He trailed off. He was not explaining it well.

"You wanted to see if I was busy," prompted Mma Ramotswe. "Is that it?"

Mr J.L.B. Matekoni nodded. "That was all I was doing."

Mma Ramotswe smiled. "You could always knock and say Ko, Ko. That is how we normally do things, is it not?"

Mr J.L.B. Matekoni took the reproach in silence. He did not wish to argue with Mma Ramotswe over this; he was keen to tell her about the butcher's car and he looked eagerly at the tea-pot. They could sit over a cup of bush tea and he would tell her about the awful thing that he had discovered quite by chance and she would tell him what to do. So he made a remark about being thirsty, as it was such a hot day, and Mma Ramotswe immediately suggested a cup of tea. She could sense that there was something on his mind and it was surely the function of a wife to listen to her husband when there was something troubling him. Not that I'm actually a wife, she told herself; I'm only a fiancée. But even then, fiancées should listen too, and could give exactly the same sort of advice as wives gave. So she put on the kettle and they had bush tea together, sitting in the shade of the acacia tree, beside Mr J.L.B. Matekoni's parked truck. And in the tree above them, an African grey dove watched them from its branch, silently, before it flew off in search of the mate which it had lost.

MMA RAMOTSWE'S reaction to Mr J.L.B. Matekoni's story was exactly as he had thought it would be. She was angry; not angry in the loud way in which some people were angry, but quietly, with only pursed lips and a particular look in her eye to show what she was feeling. She had never been able to tolerate dishonesty, which she thought threatened the very heart of relationships between people. If you could not count on other people to mean what they said, or to do what they said they would do, then life could become utterly unpredictable. The fact that we could trust one another made it possible to undertake the simple tasks of life. Everything was based on trust, even day-to-day things like crossing the road—which required trust that the drivers of cars would be paying attention—to buying the food from a roadside vendor, whom you trusted not to poison you. It was a lesson that we learned as children, when our parents threw us up into the sky and thrilled us by letting us drop into their waiting arms. We trusted those arms to be there, and they were.

Mma Ramotswe was silent for a while after Mr J.L.B. Mate-koni finished speaking. "I know that garage," she said. "A long time ago, when I first had my white van, I used to go there. That was before I started coming to Tlokweng Road Speedy Motors of course."

Mr J.L.B. Matekoni listened intently. This explained the state of the tiny white van when he had first seen it. He had assumed that the worn brake pads and the loose clutch were the results of neglect by Mma Ramotswe herself, rather than a con-sequence of the van having been looked after—if one could call it that—by First Class Motors, as it had the temerity to call itself. The thought made his heart skip a beat; it would have been so very easy for Mma Ramotswe to have had an accident as a result of her faulty brakes, and if that had happened he might never have met her and he would never have been what he was today— the fiancé of one of the finest women in Botswana. But he recog-nised that there was no point in entertaining such thoughts. History was littered with events that had changed everything and might easily not have done so. Imagine if the British had given in to South African pressure and had agreed to make what was then the Bechuanaland Protectorate into part of the Cape Province. They might easily have done that, and then there would be no Botswana today, and that would have been a loss for everybody. And his people would have suffered so much too if that had hap-pened; all those years of suffering which others had borne but which they had been spared; and all that had stood between them and that was the decision of some politician somewhere who may never even have visited the Protectorate, or cared very much. And then, of course, there was Mr Churchill, whom Mr J.L.B. Matekoni admired greatly, although he had been no more than a small boy when Mr Churchill had died. Mr J.L.B. Matekoni had read in one of Mma Makutsi's magazines that Mr

Churchill had almost been run over by a car when he was visiting America as a young man. If he had been standing six inches further into the road when the car hit him he would not have survived, and that would have made history very different, or so the article suggested. And then there was President Kennedy, who might have leaned forward just at the moment when that trigger was pulled, and might have lived to change history even more than he had already done. But Mr Churchill had survived, as had Mma Ramotswe, and that was the important thing. Now the tiny white van was scrupulously maintained, with its tight clutch and its responsive brakes. And Mr J.L.B. Matekoni had fitted a new, extra-large seat belt in the front, so that Mma Ramotswe could strap herself in without feeling uncomfortable. She was safe, which was what he wanted above all else; it would be unthinkable for anything to happen to Mma Ramotswe.

"You will have to do something about this," said Mma Ramotswe suddenly. "You cannot leave it be."

"Of course not," said Mr J.L.B. Matekoni. "I have told the butcher to bring the car round here next week, and I shall start to fix it for him. I shall have to order special parts, but I think I know where I can find them. There is a man in Mafikeng who knows all about these old cars and the parts they need. I shall ask him."

Mma Ramotswe nodded. "That will be a kind thing to do," she said. "But I was really thinking that you would have to do something about First Class Motors. They are the ones who have been cheating him. And they will be cheating others."

Mr J.L.B. Matekoni looked thoughtful. "But I don't know what I can do about them," he said. "You can't make good mechanics out of bad ones. You cannot teach a hyena to dance."

"Hyenas have nothing to do with it," said Mma Ramotswe firmly. "But jackals do. Those men in that garage are jackals. You will have to stop them."

Mr J.L.B. Matekoni felt alarmed. Mma Ramotswe was right about those mechanics, but he really did not see what he could do to stop them. There was no Chamber of Mechanics to which he could complain (Mr J.L.B. Matekoni had often thought that a Chamber of Mechanics would have been a good idea), and he had no proof that they had committed a crime. He would never be able to convince the police that fraud had been perpetrated because there would be no proof of what they had said to the butcher. They could argue that they had told him all along that they would have to put in substitute parts, and there would be many other mechanics who could go into court and testify that this was a reasonable thing for any mechanic to do in the circumstances. And if there were no help from the police, then Mr J.L.B. Matekoni would have to speak to the manager of First Class Motors, and he did not relish the prospect of that. This man had an unpleasant look on his face and was known to be something of a bully. He would not stand for allegations being made by somebody like Mr J.L.B. Matekoni, and the situation could rapidly turn threatening. It was all very well, then, for Mma Ramotswe to tell him to go and deal with the dishonest garage, but she did not understand that one could not police the motor trade single-handed.

Mr J.L.B. Matekoni said nothing. He felt that the whole day had taken an unsatisfactory turn—right from the beginning. He had encountered a shocking case of dishonesty, he had been suspected of listening in at doors (when all he had been doing was listening in), and now there was this uncomfortable expectation on the part of Mma Ramotswe that he would confront the unpleasant mechanics at First Class Motors. This was all very unsettling to a man who in general only wanted a quiet life; who liked nothing more than to be bent over the engine of a car, coaxing machinery back into working order. Everything, it seemed to him, was becoming more complicated than it need be, and—here he shuddered as the thought occurred to him—there was also hanging over him the awful threat of an involuntary parachute descent. This was far worse than anything else; a summons to a seat of judgment, an undischarged debt that sooner or later he would have to pay.

He turned to Mma Ramotswe. He should tell her now, as it would be so much easier if there was somebody to share his anxiety. She might accompany him to see Mma Potokwane to make it clear to her that there would be no parachute jump, at least not one made by him. She could handle Mma Potokwane, as women were always much better at dealing with other dominant women than were men. But when he opened his mouth to tell her, he found that the words were not there.

"Yes?" said Mma Ramotswe. "What is it, Mr J.L.B. Matekoni?"

He looked at her appealingly, willing her to help him in his torment, but Mma Ramotswe, seeing only a man staring at her with a vague longing, smiled at him and touched him gently on the cheek.

"You are a good man," she said. "And I am a very lucky woman to have such a fiancé."

Mr J.L.B. Matekoni sighed. There were cars to fix. This hill of problems could wait for its resolution until that evening when he went to Mma Ramotswe's house for dinner. That would be the time to talk, as they sat in quiet companionship on the verandah, listening to the sounds of the evening—the screeching of insects, the occasional snatch of music drifting across the waste ground behind her house, the barking of a dog somewhere in the darkness. That was when he would say, "Look, Mma Ramotswe, I am not very happy." And she would understand, because she always understood, and he had never once seen her make light of another's troubles.

But that evening, as they sat on the verandah, the children were with them, Motholeli and Puso, the two orphans whom Mr J.L.B. Matekoni had so precipitately fostered, and the moment did not seem to right to discuss these matters. So nothing was said then, nor at the kitchen table, where, as they ate the meal which Mma Ramotswe had prepared for them, the talk was all about a new dress which Motholeli had been promised and about which it seemed there was great deal to say.

CHAPTER SEVEN

EARLY MORNING AT TLOKWENG
ROAD SPEEDY MOTORS

MMA MAKUTSI woke early that day, in spite of having been to bed late and having slept very little. She had arisen at five, just before the first signs of dawn in the sky, and had gone outside to wash at the tap which she shared with two other houses. It was not ideal this sharing, and she looked forward to the day when she would have her own tap—and perhaps even a shower. This day was coming, which was one of the reasons why she had found it difficult to sleep. The previous afternoon she had found a couple of rooms to rent in another, rather better, part of town, which made up almost half—and the best half, too—of a low-cost house, and which had rudimentary plumbing all of their own. She had been told that it would not be expensive to install a simple shower, and was assured that this could be arranged within a week or two of her moving in. The information had prompted her into paying a deposit straightaway, which meant that she could make the move in little more than a week.

The rent of the new rooms was almost three times the rent which she was currently paying, but, rather to her surprise, she found that she could easily afford it. Her financial position had improved out of all recognition since she had started her part-time typing school, the Kalahari Typing School for Men. This school met several evenings a week in a church hall and offered supportive and discreet typing instruction for men. There had been many takers—she had been obliged to keep a waiting list— and the money which she had made had been carefully hus- banded. Now there was enough for the deposit and more: if she chose to empty her account, she would be able to pay at least eight months' rent and still send a substantial sum back to her family in Bobonong. She had already doubled the amount that she sent to them, and had received an appreciative letter from an aunt. "We are eating well now," her aunt had written. "You are a kind girl, and we think of you every time we eat the good food which you make it possible for us to buy. Not all girls are like you. Many are interested only in themselves (and I have a long list of such girls), but you are interested in aunties and cousins. That is a very good sign."

Mma Makutsi had smiled as she had read this letter. This aunt was a favourite of hers and one day she would pay for her to come on a visit to Gaborone. The aunt had never been out of Bobonong and it would be a great treat for her to come all the way down to Gaborone. But would it be an altogether good idea, she wondered? If you had never been anywhere in your life it could be disturbing suddenly to discover a new place. The aunt was content in Bobonong, but if she were to see how much bigger and more exciting was Gaborone, then she might find it hard to return to Bobonong, to all those rocks, and baked land, and hot sun. So perhaps the aunt would stay where she was, but Mma Makutsi could perhaps send her a picture of Gaborone, so that she would have some idea of what it was like to be in a city.

Mma Makutsi made her way out of her room and walked towards the tap at the side of the neighbouring house. She and the other people who used this tap paid the neighbour twenty pula a month for the privilege, and even then they were discouraged from using too much water. If the tap was left running while one doused one's face under it, then the owner was apt to appear and make a comment about the shortage of water in Botswana.

"We are a dry country," she had once said while Mma Makutsi was trying to wash her hair in the running water.

"Yes," said Mma Makutsi from under the stream of deliciously cool water. "That is why we have taps."

The owner had stormed off. "It is people like you," she had remarked over her shoulder, "it is people like you who are causing droughts and making all the dams empty. You be careful or the whole country will dry up and we shall have to go somewhere else. You just be careful."

This had irritated Mma Makutsi, as she was a careful user of water. But one had to turn the tap on sometimes; there was no point just standing there and looking at it, even if that is what the tap's owner would really have wanted.

This morning there was no sign of the owner, and Mma Makutsi got down on her hands and knees and allowed the water to run over her head and shoulders. After a while, she changed her position and put her feet under the water, in this way experiencing a satisfactory tingling sensation that went all the way up her calves to her knees. Then, washed and refreshed, she returned to her room. She would make breakfast now, and give her brother Richard a bowl of freshly boiled porridge . . . She stopped. For a few moments she had forgotten that Richard was no longer there, and that the corner of her room which she had curtained off for his sickbed was now empty.

Mma Makutsi stood in her doorway, looking down at the place where his bed had been. Only four months ago he had been there, struggling with the illness which was causing his life to ebb away. She had nursed him, doing her best to make him comfortable in the morning before she went off for work, and bringing him whatever small delicacies she could afford from her meagre salary. They had told her to make sure that he ate, even if his appetite was tiny. And she had done so, bringing him sticks of biltong, ruinously expensive though they were, and watermelons, which cooled his mouth and gave him the sugar that he needed.

But none of this—none of the special food, the nursing, or the love which she so generously provided—could alter the dreadful truth that the disease which was making his life so hard could never be beaten. It could be slowed down, or held in check, but it would always assert itself in the long run.

She had known, on that awful day, that he might not be there when she came back from work, because he had looked so tired, and his voice had been so reedy, like the voice of a thin bird. She had toyed with the idea of staying at home, but Mma Ramotswe was away from the office during the morning and there had to be somebody there. So she had said goodbye to him in a fairly matter-of-fact way, although she knew that this might be the last time she spoke to him, and indeed her intuition had been right. Shortly after lunchtime she had been summoned by a neighbour who looked in on him several times a morning, and she had been told to come home. Mma Ramotswe had offered to drive her back in the tiny white van, and she had accepted. As they made their way past the Botswana Technical College, she had suddenly felt that it was too late, and she had sat back in her seat, her head sunk in her hands, knowing what she would find when she arrived at her room.

Sister Banjule was there. She was the nurse from the Anglican Hospice and the neighbour had known to call her too. She was sitting by his bedside, and when Mma Makutsi came in she rose to her feet and put her arm around her, as did Mma Ramotswe.

"He said your name," she whispered to Mma Makutsi. "That is what he said before the Lord took him. I am telling you the truth. That is what he said."

They stood together for several minutes, the three women; Sister Banjule in the white uniform of her calling, Mma Ramotswe in her red dress, that she would now change for black, and Mma Makutsi in the new blue dress that she had treated herself to with some of the proceeds of the typing school classes. And then the neighbour, who had been standing near the door, led Mma Makutsi away so that Sister Banjule could ensure in private the last dignities for a man whose life had not amounted to much, but who now received, as of right, the unconditional love of one who knew how to give just that. *Receive the soul of our brother, Richard,* said Sister Banjule as she gently took from the body its stained and threadbare shirt and replaced it with a garment of white, that a poor man might leave this world in cleanliness and light.

SHE WISHED that he could have seen her new place, as he would have appreciated the space and the privacy. He would have loved the tap too, and she would have probably ended up being as bad as the woman who watched the water, telling him off for using too much. But that was not to be, and she accepted that, because she knew now that his suffering was at an end.

The new place, when she moved into it, would be much closer to work. It was not far from the African Mall, in an area which everybody called Extension Two. The streets there were nothing like Zebra Drive, which was leafy and quiet, but at least they were recognisably streets, with names of their own, rather than being the rutted tracks which dodged this way and that round Naledi. And the houses there were neatly set in the middle of small plots of land, with paw-paw trees or flowering bushes dotted about the yards. These houses, although small, were suitable for clerks, or the managers of small stores, or even teachers. It was not at all inappropriate that somebody of her status—a graduate of the Botswana Secretarial College and an assistant detective—should live in a place like that, and she felt proud when she thought of her impending move. There would be less smell, too, which would be good, as there were proper drains and not so much litter. Not that Botswana smelled; anything but, though there were small corners of it—one of these near Mma Makutsi's room—where one was reminded of humanity and heat.

The fact that Mma Makutsi had two rooms in a house of four rooms meant, in her mind, that she could say that she would now be living in a house. *My house*—she tried the words out, and at first they seemed strange, almost meretricious. But it was true; she would shortly be responsible for half a roof and half a yard, and that justified the expression *my house*. It was a comforting thought—anther milestone on the road that had led her from that constrained life in Bobonong, with its non-existent possibilities and its utter isolation, via the Botswana Secretarial College, with its crowning moment of the award of ninety-seven per cent in the final examinations, to the anticipated elevation to the status of householder, with a yard, and paw-paw trees of her own, and a place where the washing could be hung out to dry in the wind.

The furnishing and decoration of the new house was a matter of the utmost importance, and had been the subject of lengthy discussion with Mma Ramotswe. There were long hours at the office when nothing very much happened, and these might be spent in conversation, or crocheting perhaps, or in simply looking up at the ceiling, with its little fly tracks, like miniature paths through the bush. Mma Ramotswe had strong views on the subject of decoration, and had put these into effect in the house on Zebra Drive, where the living room was unquestionably the most comfortable room Mma Makutsi had ever seen. When she had first visited Mma Ramotswe at home, Mma Makutsi had stood for a moment in the living room doorway, marvelling at the matching suite of sofa and chairs, with their thick cushions, so inviting for a tired or discouraged person, and at the treasures on the shelves—the commemorative plate of Sir Seretse Khama and the Queen Elizabeth II tea cup, with the Queen smiling out in such a reassuring way; and the framed picture of Nelson Mandela with the late King Moshoeshoe II of Lesotho; and the illuminated motto which called for peace and understanding in the house. She had stood there and realised that there had been little beauty in her life; that she had never had a room which in any way expressed her striving for something better, but that perhaps one day she would. And now it was happening.

Mma Ramotswe had been generous. When she first heard of the move, she had taken Mma Makutsi to the house on Zebra Drive and she had gone through the whole place, room by room, identifying household effects which she could pass on to her assistant. There was a chair which nobody used any more, but which had a bright red seat. She could have that. And then there were the yellow curtains, which had been replaced by a new set; Mma Makutsi had scarcely dared to ask for those, but they had been offered, and she had accepted with alacrity.

Now, sitting at her desk in the morning, it seemed to her that her life could hardly get any better. There was her new home to look forward to, furnished in part with Mma Ramotswe's generous gifts; there was the prospect of having a little spare money in her pocket, rather than having to count every thebe; and there was the knowledge that she had a good job, with good people, and that her work made things better, at least for some. Since she had started at the No. 1 Ladies' Detective Agency, she had managed to help quite a number of clients. They had gone away feeling the better for what she had done for them, and that, more than any fee, made her work worthwhile. So those glamorous girls who had gone to work in those companies with new offices; those girls who had never achieved much more than fifty per cent in the examinations at the Botswana Secretarial College; those girls may have highly paid jobs, *but did they enjoy their work*? Mma Makutsi was sure that they did not. They sat at their desks, pretending to type, watching the hands of the clock approach five. And then, exactly on the hour, they disappeared, eager to get as far away as possible from their offices. Well, it was not like that for Mma Makutsi. Sometimes she would be there in the office well after six, or even seven. Occasionally she found that she was so absorbed in what she was doing that she would not even notice that it had become dark, and when she walked home it would be through the night, with all its sounds and the smells of woodsmoke from cooking fires, and with the sky up above like a great black blanket.

Mma Makutsi rose from her chair and went to look out of the window. Charlie, the older apprentice, was getting out of a minibus which had drawn off the main road. He waved to somebody who remained inside, and then began to walk towards the garage, his hands stuck in his pockets, his lips moving as he whistled one of those irritating tunes which he picked up. Just as he reached the garage, he began a few steps of a dance, and Mma Makutsi grimaced. He was thinking of girls, of course, as he always did. That explained the dance.

She drew back from the window, shaking her head. She knew that the apprentices were popular with girls, but she could not imagine what anybody saw in them. It was not that they had much to talk about—cars and girls seemed to be their only interest—and yet there were plenty of girls who were prepared to gig-gle and flirt with them. Perhaps those girls were in their own way as bad as the apprentices themselves, being interested only in boys and make-up. There were plenty of girls like that, Mma Makutsi thought, and maybe they would make very good wives for these apprentices when they were ready to marry.

The door, which was ajar, was now opened and the appren-tice stuck his head round.

"Dumela, Mma," he said. "You have slept well?"

"Dumela, Rra," Mma Makutsi replied. "Yes, I have. Thank you. I was here very early and I have been thinking."

The apprentice smiled. "You must not think too much, Mma," he said. "It is not good for women to think too much."

Mma Makutsi decided to ignore this remark, but after a moment she had to reply. She could not let this sort of thing go unanswered; he would never have said something like that if Mma Ramotswe had been present, and if he thought that he could get away with it then she would have to disabuse him of that idea.

"It is not good for men if women think too much," she retorted. "Oh yes, you are right there. If women start thinking about how useless some men are, then it is bad for men in gen-eral. Oh yes, that is true."

"That is not what I meant," said the apprentice.

"Hah!" said Mma Makutsi. "So now you are changing your mind. You did not know what you were saying because your tongue is out of control. It is always walking away on its own and leaving your head behind. Perhaps there is some medicine for that. Maybe there is an operation that can fix it for you!"

The apprentice looked cross. He knew that there was no point in trying to better Mma Makutsi in an argument, but any-way he had not come into the office to argue; he had come in to impart some very important news.

"I have read something in the paper," he said. "I have read something very interesting."

Mma Makutsi glanced at the paper which he had extracted from his pocket. Already it had been smudged with greasy finger-prints, and she wrinkled her nose in distaste.

"There is something about Mr J.L.B. Matekoni in here," said the apprentice. "It is on the front page."

Mma Makutsi drew in her breath. Had something happened to Mr J.L.B. Matekoni? Newspapers were full of bad news about people, and she wondered whether something unpleasant had happened to Mr J.L.B. Matekoni. Or perhaps Mr J.L.B. Matekoni had been arrested for something or other; no, that was impossible. Nobody would ever arrest Mr J.L.B. Matekoni. He was the last person who would ever do anything that would send him to jail. They would have to arrest the whole population of Botswana before they got to Mr J.L.B. Matekoni.

The apprentice, relishing the interest which his comment had aroused, unfolded the newspaper and handed it to Mma Makutsi. "There," he said. "The Boss is going to do something really brave. Ow! I'm glad that it's him and not me!"

Mma Makutsi took the newspaper and began to read. "Mr J.L.B. Matekoni, proprietor of Tlokweng Road Speedy Motors, and a well-known figure in the Gaborone motor trade," began the report, "has agreed to perform a parachute jump to raise money for the Tlokweng orphan farm. Mma Silvia Potokwane, the matron of the orphan farm, said that Mr J.L.B. Matekoni made the surprise offer only a few days ago. She expects him to be able to raise at least five thousand pula in sponsorship. Sponsorship forms have already been distributed and many sponsors are coming forward."

She read the report aloud, the apprentice standing before her and smiling.

"You see," said the apprentice. "None of us would have imagined that the Boss would be so brave, and there he is planning to jump out of an aeroplane. And all to help the orphan farm! Isn't that good of him?"

"Yes," said Mma Makutsi. It was very kind, but she had immediately wondered what Mma Ramotswe would think of her fiancé making a parachute jump. If she had a fiancé herself, then she was not sure whether she would approve of that; indeed the more she thought about it the more she realised that she would not approve. Parachute jumps went wrong; everybody knew that.

"They go wrong, these parachute jumps," said the apprentice, as if he had picked up the direction of her thoughts. "There was a man in the Botswana Defence Force whose parachute didn't open. That man is late now."

"That is very sad," said Mma Makutsi. "I am sorry for that man."

"The other men were watching from the ground," the apprentice continued. "They looked up and shouted to him to open his emergency parachute—they always carry two, you see—but he did not hear them."

Mma Makutsi looked at the apprentice. What did he mean: *he didn't hear them?* Of course he wouldn't hear them. This was typical of the curious, ill-informed way in which the apprentices, and so many young men like them, viewed the world. It was astonishing to think that they had been to school, and yet there they were, with a good Cambridge Certificate. As Mma Ramotswe pointed out, it must be very difficult being the Minister of Education and having to deal with raw material like this.

"But he would never be able to hear them," said Mma Makutsi. "They were wasting their breath."

"Yes," said the apprentice. "It is possible that he had fallen asleep."

Mma Makutsi sighed. "You would not fall asleep while you were jumping from an aeroplane. That doesn't happen."

"Oh yes?" challenged the apprentice. "And what about falling asleep at the wheel—while you're driving? I saw a car go off the Francistown Road once, just because of that. The driver had gone to sleep and the next thing he knew he had hit a tree and the car rolled over. You can go to sleep anywhere."

"Driving is different," said Mma Makutsi. "You do that for a long time. You become hot and drowsy. But when you jump out of an aeroplane, you are not likely to feel hot and drowsy. You will not go to sleep."

"How do you know?" said the apprentice. "Have you jumped out of an aeroplane, Mma? Hah! You would have to watch your skirt! All the boys would be standing down below and whistling because your skirt would be over your head. Hah!"

Mma Makutsi shook her head. "It is no good talking to somebody like you," she said. "And anyway, here's Mr J.L.B. Matekoni's truck. We can ask him about this parachute business. We can find out if what the paper says is true."

MR J.L.B. Matekoni parked his truck in the shade under the acacia tree beside the garage, making sure to leave enough room for Mma Ramotswe to park her tiny white van when she arrived. She would not arrive until nine o'clock, she had told him, because she was taking Motholeli to the doctor. Dr Moffat had telephoned to say that a specialist was visiting the hospital and that he had agreed to see Motholeli. "I do not think that he will be able to say much more than we have said," Dr Moffat had warned. "But there's no harm in his seeing her." And Dr Moffat had been right; nothing new could be said.

Mr J.L.B. Matekoni was pleased that he was getting to know

the children better. He had always been slightly puzzled by children, and felt that he did not really understand them. There were children all round Botswana, of course, and nobody could be unaware of them, but he had been surprised at how these orphans thought about things. The boy, Puso, was a case in point. He was behaving very much better than he had in the past—and Mr J.L.B. Matekoni was thankful for that—but he was still inclined to be on the moody side. Sometimes, when he was driving with Mr J.L.B. Matekoni in his truck, he would sit there, staring out of the window, and saying nothing at all.

"What are you thinking of?" Mr J.L.B. Matekoni would ask, and Puso would shake his head and reply, "Nothing."

That could not be true. Nobody thought of nothing, but it was difficult to imagine what thoughts a boy of that age would have. What did boys do? Mr J.L.B. Matekoni tried to remember what he had done as a boy, but there was a curious gap, as if he had done nothing at all. This was strange, he thought. Mma Ramotswe remembered everything about her childhood and was always describing the details of events which had happened all those years ago. But when he tried to do that, Mr J.L.B. Matekoni could not even remember the names of the other boys in his class, apart from one or two very close friends with whom he had kept in touch. And it was the same with the initiation school, when all the boys were sent off to be inducted into the traditions of men. That was a great moment in your life, and you were meant to remember it, but he had only the vaguest memories.

Engines were different, of course. Although his memory for people's names and for people themselves was not terribly good, Mr J.L.B. Matekoni remembered virtually every engine that he had ever handled, from the large and loyal diesels which he had learned to deal with during his apprenticeship to the clinically efficient, and characterless, motors of modern cars. And not only did he remember the distinguished engines—such as that which powered the British High Commissioner's car—but he also remembered their more modest brothers, such as that which drove the only NSU Prinz which he had ever seen on the roads of Botswana; a humble car, indeed, which looked the same from the front or the back and which had an engine very like the motor on Mma Ramotswe's sewing machine. All of these engines were like old friends to Mr J.L.B. Matekoni—old friends with all the individual quirks which old friends inevitably had, but which were so comfortable and reassuring.

Mr J.L.B. Matekoni got out of his truck and stretched his limbs. He had a busy day ahead of him, with four cars booked in for a routine service, and another which would require the replacement of the servo system on its brakes. This was a tricky procedure, because it was difficult to get at in the first place, and then, when one got there, it was very easy to replace incorrectly. The problem, as Mr J.L.B. Matekoni had explained to the apprentices on numerous occasions, was that the ends of the brake pipes were flared and one had to put a small nut into these flared ends. This nut allowed you to connect the servo mechanism to the pipes, but, and this was the real danger, if you cross-threaded the nuts you would get a leak. And if you avoided this danger, but if you were too rough, then you could twist a brake pipe. That was a terrible thing to do, as it meant that you had to replace the entire brake pipe, and these pipes, as everybody knew, ran through the body of the car like arteries. The apprentices had caused both of these disasters in the past, and he had been obliged to spend almost a whole day sorting things out. Now he no longer trusted them to do it. They could watch if they wished, but they would not be allowed to touch. This was the main problem with the apprentices; they had the necessary theoretical knowledge, or some of it, but so often they were slipshod in the way they finished a job—as if they had become bored with it—and Mr J.L.B. Matekoni knew that you could never be slipshod when it came to brake pipes.

He went into the garage and, hearing voices from the detective agency, he knocked on the door and looked in to see Mma Makutsi handing Charlie a folded-up newspaper. They turned and stared at him.

"Here's the Boss," said the apprentice. "Here's the brave man himself."

"The hero," echoed Mma Makutsi, smiling.

Mr J.L.B. Matekoni frowned. "What is this?" he asked. "Why are you calling me a brave man?"

"Not just us," said the apprentice, handing him the newspaper. "The whole town will be calling you brave now."

Mr J.L.B. Matekoni took the newspaper. It can only be one thing, he thought, and as his eye fell upon the article his fears were confirmed. He stood there, his hands shaking slightly as he held the offending newspaper, the dismay mounting within him. This was Mma Potokwane's doing. Nobody else could have told the newspaper about the parachute jump, as he had spoken to nobody about it. She had no right to do this, he thought. She had no right at all.

"Is it true?" asked Mma Makutsi. "Did you really say that you would jump out of an aeroplane?"

"Of course he did," exclaimed the apprentice. "The Boss is a brave man."

"Well," began Mr J.L.B. Matekoni, "Mma Potokwane said to me that I should and then . . ."

"Oh!" said Mma Makutsi, clapping her hands with delight. "So it is true then! This is very exciting. I will sponsor you, Rra. Yes, I will sponsor you up to thirty pula!"

"Why do you say 'up to'?" asked the apprentice.

"Because that's what these sponsorship forms normally say," said Mma Makutsi. "You put down a maximum amount."

"But that's only because when a person is doing something like a sponsored walk they may not reach the end," said the apprentice. "In the case of a parachute jump, the person you have sponsored usually reaches the end—one way or the other." He laughed at his observation, but Mr J.L.B. Matekoni merely stared at him.

Mma Makutsi was annoyed with the apprentice. It was not right to make remarks like that in the presence of one who would be taking such a great personal risk for a good cause. "You must not talk like that," she said severely. "This is not a joke for you to laugh at. This is a brave thing that Mr J.L.B. Matekoni is doing."

"Oh it's brave all right," said the apprentice. "It is surely a brave thing, Mma. Look what happened to that poor Botswana Defence Force man . . ."

"What happened to him?" asked Mr J.L.B. Matekoni.

Mma Makutsi glowered at the apprentice. "Oh that has nothing to do with you, Mr J.L.B. Matekoni," she said quickly. "That is another thing. We do not need to talk about that thing."

Mr J.L.B. Matekoni looked doubtful. "But he said that something happened to a Botswana Defence Force man. What is that thing?"

"It is not an important thing," said Mma Makutsi. "Sometimes the Botswana Defence Force makes silly mistakes. It is only human after all."

"How do you know it was the Defence Force's mistake?" interjected the apprentice. "How do you know that it wasn't that man's fault?"

"What man?" asked Mr. J.L.B. Matekoni.

"I do not know his name," said Mma Makutsi. "And anyway, I

am tired of talking about these things. I want to get some work done before Mma Ramotswe comes in. There is a letter here which we shall have to reply to. There is a lot to do."

The apprentice smiled. "All right," he said. "I am also busy, Mma. You are not the only one." He gave a small jump, which could have been the beginnings of one of his dances, but which also could have been just a small jump. Then he left the office.

Mma Makutsi returned to her desk in a businesslike fashion. "I have drawn up the accounts for last month," she said. "It was a much better month."

"Good," said Mr J.L.B. Matekoni. "Now about this Defence Force man . . ."

He did not finish, as Mma Makutsi interrupted him with a screech. "Oh," she cried, "I have forgotten something. Oh, I am very stupid. Sorry, Mr J.L.B. Matekoni, I have forgotten to enter those receipts over there. I am going to have to check everything."

Mr J.L.B. Matekoni shrugged. There was something which she did not want him to be told, but he thought that he knew exactly what it was. It was about a parachute that had not opened.

CHAPTER EIGHT

TEA IS ALWAYS THE SOLUTION

MMA RAMOTSWE swept up to the premises of Tlokweng Road Speedy Motors, bringing her tiny white van to a halt under the acacia tree. She had been thinking as she drove in, not of work, but of the children, who were proving such surprising people to live with. Children were never simple—she knew that—but she had always assumed that brothers and sisters had at least something in common in their tastes and behaviour. Yet here were these two orphans, who were children of the same mother and same father (or so Mma Potokwane had told her) and yet who were so thoroughly different. Motholeli was interested in cars and trucks, and liked nothing better than to watch Mr J.L.B. Matekoni with his spanners and wrenches and all the other mysterious tools of his calling. She was adamant that she would be a mechanic, in spite of her wheelchair and in spite of the fact that her arms were not as strong as the arms of other girls of her age. The illness which had deprived her of the use of her legs had touched at other parts of her body too, weakening the muscles and sometimes constricting her chest and lungs. She never complained, of course, as it was not in her nature to do so, but Mma Ramotswe could tell when a momentary shadow of discomfort passed over her face, and her heart went out to the brave, uncomplaining girl whom Mr J.L.B. Matekoni, almost by accident, had brought into her life. Puso, the boy, whom Motholeli had rescued from burial with their mother, scraping the hot sand from his face and breathing air into his struggling lungs, shared none of his sister's interest in machinery. He was indifferent to cars, except as a means of getting around, and he was happiest in his own company, playing in the patch of scrub bush behind Mma Ramotswe's house in Zebra Drive, throwing stones at lizards or tricking those minute creatures known as ant lions into showing themselves. These insects, small as ticks but quicker and more energetic, created little conical wells in the sand, snares for any ants that might wander that way. Once on the edge of the trap, the ant would inevitably trigger a miniature landslide, tumbling down the sides of it. The ant lion, hidden under grains of sand at the bottom, would burrow out and seize its prey, dragging it back underground to provide a tasty meal. If you were a boy, and so minded, you could tickle the edge of the trap with a blade of grass and create a false alarm to bring the ant lion out of its lair. Then you could flip it out with a twig and witness its confusion. That was an entertaining pastime for a boy, and Puso liked to do this for hours on end.

Mma Ramotswe had imagined that he would play with other boys, but he seemed to be quite happy on his own. She had invited a friend to send her sons over, and these boys had arrived, but Puso had simply stared at them and said nothing.

"You should talk to these boys," Mma Ramotswe admonished him. "They are your guests, and you should talk to them."

He had mumbled something, and they had gone off into the garden together, but when she had looked out of the window a few minutes later, Mma Ramotswe had seen the two visiting boys entertaining themselves by climbing a tree while Puso busied himself with a nest of white ants which he had found underneath a mopipi tree.

"Leave him to do what he wants to do," Mr J.LB. Matekoni had advised her. "Remember where he comes from. Remember his people."

Mma Ramotswe knew exactly what he meant. These children, although not pure-bred Masarwa, had at least some of that blood in their veins. It was easy to forget that, because they did not look like bushmen, and yet here was the boy taking this strange, almost brooding interest in the bush and in creatures that most other people would not ever notice. That, she imagined, was because he had been given the eyes to see these things; as we are given the eyes of those who have gone before us, and can see the world in the way in which they saw it. In her case, she knew that she had her father's eye for cattle, and could tell their quality in an instant, at first glance. That was something she just knew—she just knew it. Perhaps Mr J.L.B. Matekoni could do the same with cars; one glance, and he would know.

She got out of the tiny white van and walked round the side of the building to the door that led directly into the No. 1 Ladies' Detective Agency. She could tell that they were busy in the garage, and she did not want to disturb them. In an hour or so it would be time for tea-break, and she could chat to Mr J.L.B. Matekoni then. In the meantime there was a letter to sign— Mma Makutsi had started to type it yesterday—and there might be new mail to go through. And sooner or later she would have to begin the investigation of Mma Holonga's list of suitors. She had no idea how she was going to tackle that, but Mma Makutsi might be able to come up with a suggestion. Mma Makutsi had a good mind—as her ninety-seven per cent at the Botswana Secretarial College had demonstrated to the world—but she was inclined to unrealistic schemes. Sometimes these worked, but on other occasions Mma Ramotswe had been obliged to pour cold water on over-ambitious ideas.

She entered the office to find Mma Makutsi polishing her large spectacles, staring up at the ceiling as she did so. This was always a sign that she was thinking, and Mma Ramotswe wondered what she was thinking about. Perhaps the morning post, which Mma Makutsi now picked up from the post office on her way into work, had contained an interesting letter, possibly from a new client. Or perhaps it had brought one of those anonymous letters which people inexplicably sent them; letters of denunciation which the senders thought that they would be interested to receive, but which were no business of theirs. Such letters were usually mundane, revealing nothing but human pettiness and jealousy. But sometimes they contained a snippet of information which was genuinely interesting, or gave an insight into the strange corners of people's lives. Mma Makutsi could be thinking about one of these, thought Mma Ramotswe, or she could just be staring at the ceiling because there was nothing else to do. Sometimes, when people stared, there was nothing else in their minds, and all they were doing was thinking of the ceiling, or of the trees, or of the sky, or of any of the things that it was so satisfying just to stare at.

"You're thinking of something, Mma," said Mma Ramotswe. "Whenever I see you polishing your glasses like that, I know that you are thinking of something."

Mma Makutsi looked round sharply, disturbed by the sudden sound of her employer's voice. "You surprised me, Mma," she said. "I was sitting here and I suddenly heard your voice. It made me jump."

Mma Ramotswe smiled. "Mr J.L.B. Matekoni says that I creep up on him too. But I do not mean to do that." She paused. "So what were you thinking about, Mma?"

Mma Makutsi replaced her glasses and adjusted their position on the bridge of her nose. She had been thinking about Mr J.L.B. Matekoni and his parachute drop and about how Mma Ramotswe would react to the news, that is assuming that she had not heard it already.

"Have you seen the paper today?" she asked.

Mma Ramotswe shook her head as she walked over to her desk. "I have not seen it," she said. "I have been busy taking the children here and there. I have had no time to sit down." She threw Mma Makutsi a quizzical glance. "Is there something special in it?"

So she does not know, thought Mma Makutsi. Well, she would have to tell her, and it would probably be a shock for her.

"Mr J.L.B. Matekoni is going to jump," she said. "It is in the paper this morning."

Mma Ramotswe stared at Mma Makutsi. What was she talking about? What was this nonsense about Mr J.L.B. Matekoni jumping?

"Out of a plane," went on Mma Makutsi quickly. "Mr J.L.B. Matekoni is going to do a parachute jump."

Mma Ramotswe laughed. "What nonsense!" she said. "Mr J.L.B. Matekoni would never do something like that. Who has put such nonsense in the newspapers?"

"It's true," said Mma Makutsi. "It's one of these charity jumps. Mma Potokwane . . ."

She had to say no more. At the mention of Mma Potokwane's name, Mma Ramotswe's expression changed. "Mma Potokwane?" she said sharply. "She has been forcing Mr J.L.B. Matekoni to do things again? A parachute jump?"

Mma Makutsi nodded. "It is in the paper," she said. "And I have spoken to Mr J.L.B. Matekoni myself. He has confirmed that it is true."

Mma Ramotswe sat quite still. For a moment she said nothing, as the implications of Mma Makutsi's revelations sank in. Then she thought, I shall be a widow. I shall be a widow before I am even married.

Mma Makutsi could see the effect the news was having on Mma Ramotswe and she searched for words that might help.

"I don't think he wants to do it," she said quietly. "But now he is trapped. Mma Potokwane has told the newspapers."

Mma Ramotswe said nothing, while Mma Makutsi continued. "You must go into the garage right now," she said. "You must put a stop to it. You must forbid him. It is too dangerous."

Mma Ramotswe nodded. "I do not think that it is a good idea. But I'm not sure that I can forbid him. He is not a child."

"But you are his wife," said Mma Makutsi. "Or you are almost his wife. You have the right to stop him doing something dangerous."

Mma Ramotswe frowned. "No, I do not have that right. I can talk to him about it, but if you try to stop people from doing things they can resent it. I do not want Mr J.L.B. Matekoni to think that I am telling him what to do all the time. That is not a good start for a marriage."

"But it hasn't started yet," protested Mma Makutsi. "You are just an engaged lady. And you've been an engaged lady for a long time now. There is no sign of a wedding." She stopped, realising that perhaps she had gone too far. What she said was quite true, but it did not help to draw attention to their long engagement and to the conspicuous absence of any wedding plans.

Mma Ramotswe was not offended. "You are right," she said. "I am a very engaged lady. I have been waiting for a long time. But you cannot push men around. They do not like it. They like to feel that they are making their own decisions."

"Even when they are not?" interjected Mma Makutsi.

"Yes," said Mma Ramotswe. "We all know that it is women who take the decisions, but we have to let men think that the decisions are theirs. It is an act of kindness on the part of women."

Mma Makutsi took off her glasses and polished them on her lace handkerchief, now threadbare but so loved. This was the handkerchief that she had bought when she was at the Botswana Secretarial College, at a time when she had virtually nothing else, and it meant a great deal to her.

"So we should say nothing at the moment?" she said. "And then . . ."

"And then we find a chance to say something very small," said Mma Ramotswe. "We shall find some way to get Mr J.L.B. Matekoni out of this. But it will be done carefully, and he will think that he has changed his mind."

Mma Makutsi smiled. "You are very clever with men, Mma. You know how their minds work."

Mma Ramotswe shrugged. "When I was a girl I used to watch little boys playing and I saw what they did. Now that I am a lady, I know that there is not much difference. Boys and men are the same people, in different clothes. Boys wear short trousers and men wear long trousers. But they are just the same if you take their trousers off."

Mma Makutsi stared at Mma Ramotswe, who, suddenly flustered, added quickly, "That is not what I meant to say. What I meant to say is that trousers mean nothing. Men think like boys, and if you understand boys, then you understand men. That is what I meant to say."

"I thought so," said Mma Makutsi. "I did not think that you meant anything else."

"Good," said Mma Ramotswe briskly. "Then let us have a cup of tea and think about how we are going to deal with this problem which Mma Holonga brought us the other day. We cannot sit here all day talking about men. We must get down to work. There is much to do."

Mma Makutsi made the bush tea and they sipped on the dark red liquid as they discussed the best approach to the issue of Mma Holonga's suitors. Tea, of course, made the problem seem smaller, as it always does, and by the time they reached the bottom of their cups, and Mma Makutsi had reached for the slightly chipped tea-pot to pour a refill, it had become clear what they would have to do.

CHAPTER NINE

HOW TO HANDLE YOUNG MEN THROUGH THE APPLICATION OF PSYCHOLOGY

A T THE end of that day's work Mma Ramotswe so engineered matters that she was standing at the door of her tiny white van at precisely the time—one minute to five—that the two apprentices came out of the garage entrance, wiping their greasy hands on a handful of the loose white lint provided by Mr J.L.B. Matekoni. Mr J.L.B. Matekoni knew all about oil-dermatitis, the condition which stalked mechanics and which had struck several of his brother mechanics over the years, and he made every effort to drum the lesson into the heads of his apprentices. Not that this worked, of course; they were still inclined to limit themselves to a quick plunge of the hands into a bucket of lukewarm water, but at least on occasion they resorted to lint and made some effort to do it properly. There was an old barrel for the used lint, and for other detritus of their calling, but they tended to ignore this and now Mma Ramotswe saw the lint tossed casually to the ground. As they did so, the older apprentice looked up and saw her watching them. He muttered something to his friend, and they dutifully picked up the lint and walked off to deposit it in the barrel.

"You are very tidy," called out Mma Ramotswe when they re-emerged. "Mr J.L.B. Matekoni will be pleased."

"We were going to put it there anyway," said the younger apprentice reproachfully. "You don't have to tell us to do it, Mma."

"Yes," said Mma Ramotswe. "I knew that. I thought perhaps you had just dropped it by mistake. That sometimes happens, doesn't it? I have often seen you drop things by mistake. Sweet papers. Chip bags. Newspapers."

The apprentices, who had now drawn level with the tiny white van, looked at their shoes sheepishly. They were no match for Mma Ramotswe, and they knew it.

"But I don't want to talk about litter," said Mma Ramotswe kindly. "I can see that you have been working very hard today, and I thought I would drive you both home. It will save you waiting for a minibus."

"You are very kind, Mma," said the older apprentice.

Mma Ramotswe gestured to the passenger seat. "You sit in there, Charlie. You are the older one. And you," she looked at the younger apprentice and pointed to the back of the van, "you can go there. Next time you can ride in front."

She had a rough idea where the two young men lived. The younger one stayed with his uncle in a house beyond the Francis-town Road brewery and the older one lodged with an aunt and uncle near the orphan farm at Tlokweng. It would take over half an hour to deliver them both, and the children would be waiting for her at home, but this was important and she would do it cheerfully.

She would deliver the younger one first, skirting the edge of the town, driving past the university and the Sun Hotel and the road to Maru-a-Pula. Then Nyerere Drive bore left, past the end of Elephant Road, and ran down to Nelson Mandela Drive, which she still thought of as the old Francistown Road. They crossed the dry course of the Segoditshane River and then the older apprentice directed her to a side road lined by a row of small, well-kept houses.

"That is his uncle's place over there," he said, pointing to one of the houses. "He lives in that shack on the side. That is where he sleeps, but he eats inside with the family."

They stopped outside the gate and the younger apprentice jumped out of the van and clapped his hands in gratitude. Mma Ramotswe smiled and said through the open window, "I am glad that I saved you a walk." Then she waved and they drove off.

"He is a good boy," said Mma Ramotswe. "He will make a good husband for some girl one day."

"Hah!" said the older apprentice. "That girl will have to catch him first. He is a quick runner, that boy. It will not be easy for the girls!"

Mma Ramotswe pretended to look interested. "But what if a very beautiful girl with lots of money saw him? What then? Surely he would like to marry a girl like that and have a large car? Perhaps even one of those German cars that you think are so smart. What then?"

The apprentice laughed. "Oh, I would marry a girl like that double-quick. But girls like that won't look at boys like us. We are just apprentice mechanics. Girls like that want boys from rich families or with very good jobs. Accountants. People like that. We just get ordinary girls."

Mma Ramotswe clucked her tongue. "Oh! That is very sad. It is a pity that you don't know how to attract more glamorous girls. It is a great pity." She paused before saying, almost as an aside, "I could tell you, of course."

The apprentice looked at her incredulously. "You, Mma? You could tell me how to attract that sort of girl?"

"Of course I could," said Mma Ramotswe. "I am a woman,

remember? I used to be a girl. I know how girls think. Just because I am a bit older now and I do not run round looking at boys doesn't mean that I have forgotten how girls think."

The apprentice raised an eyebrow. "You tell me then," he said. "You tell me this secret."

Mma Ramotswe was silent. This, she thought, was the difficult part. She had to make sure that the apprentice would take what she had to say seriously, and that meant that she should not be too quick to impart the information.

"I don't know whether I should tell you," she said. "I cannot just tell anybody. I would only want to tell a man who would be kind to these glamorous girls. Just because they are glamorous doesn't mean that they do not have their feelings. Maybe I should wait a few years before I tell you."

The apprentice, who had been smiling, now frowned. "I would treat such a girl very well, Mma. You can count on me."

Mma Ramotswe concentrated on her driving. There was an elderly man on a bicycle ahead of them, a battered hat perched on his head, and a red hen tied to the carrier on the back of his cycle. She slowed down, giving him a wide berth.

"That hen is making its last journey," she said. "He will be taking it to somebody who will eat it."

The apprentice glanced behind him. "That is what happens to all hens. That is what they are for."

"They may not think that," said Mma Ramotswe.

The apprentice laughed. "They cannot think. They have very small heads. There are no brains in a chicken."

"What is in their heads, then?" asked Mma Ramotswe.

"There is just blood and some bits of meat," said the apprentice. "I have seen it. There is no brain."

Mma Ramotswe nodded. "Oh," she said. There was no point

in arguing with these boys about matters of this sort; they were usually quite adamant that they were right, even if there was no basis for what they said.

"But what is this thing about girls?" the apprentice persisted. "You can tell me, Mma. I may talk about girls a lot, but I am very kind to them. You ask Mr J.L.B. Matekoni. He has seen how well I treat girls."

They were now nearing the Tlokweng Road, and Mma Ramotswe thought that the time was ripe. She had aroused the apprentice's attention and now he was listening to her.

"Well then," she began, "I will tell you a very certain way to attract the attention of one of these glamorous girls. You must become well-known. If you are well-known—if your name is in the papers—then these girls cannot resist you. You look about you and see what sort of man has that sort of lady. It is always the ones who are in the papers. They get those girls every time."

The apprentice looked immediately defeated. "That is not good news for me," he said. "I shall never be well-known. I shall never get into the papers."

"Why not?" asked Mma Ramotswe. "Why give up before you have started?"

"Because nobody is ever going to write about me," said the apprentice. "I am just an unknown person. I am not going to be famous."

"But look at Mr J.L.B. Matekoni," said Mma Ramotswe. "Look at him. He was in the papers today. Now he is well-known."

"That is different," the apprentice retorted. "He is in the papers because he is going to do a parachute jump."

"But you could do that," said Mma Ramotswe, as if the idea had just occurred. "If you were to jump out of an aeroplane you would be all over the papers and the glamorous girls would notice all right. They would be all over you. I know how these girls think."

"But . . ." began the apprentice.

He did not finish. "Oh yes they would," Mma Ramotswe went on. "There is nothing—nothing—that they like more than bravery. If you jumped out of the plane—maybe instead of Mr J.L.B. Matekoni, who is possibly too old to do that these days—then you would be the one who would get all the attention. I guarantee it. Those girls would be waiting for you. You could take your pick. You could choose the one with the biggest car."

"If she had the biggest car then she would also have the biggest bottom," said the apprentice, smiling. "She would need a big car to fit her bottom in. Such a girl would be very nice."

Mma Ramotswe would normally not have let such a remark pass without a sharp retort, but this was not the occasion, and she simply smiled. "It seems simple to me," she said. "You do the jump. You get the girl. It's perfectly safe."

The apprentice thought for a moment. "But what about that Botswana Defence Force man? The one whose parachute didn't open. What about him?"

Mma Ramotswe shook her head. "You are wrong there, Charlie. His parachute would have opened *if he had pulled the cord*. You yourself said to Mma Makutsi that that man had probably gone to sleep. There was nothing wrong with his parachute, you see. You are much cleverer than that man. You will not forget to pull the cord."

The apprentice thought for a moment. "And you think that the papers will write about me?"

"Of course they will," said Mma Ramotswe. "I shall get Mma Potokwane to talk to them again. She is always giving them stories about the orphan farm. She will tell them to put a big photograph of you on the front page. That will certainly be read by the sort of girl we are talking about."

Mma Ramotswe slowed down. A small herd of donkeys had wandered onto the road ahead of them and had stopped in the middle, looking at the tiny white van as if they had never before encountered a vehicle. She brought the van to a halt, glancing quickly at the apprentice as she did so. Psychology, she thought; that is what they called it these days, but in her view it was something much older than that. It was woman's knowledge, that was what it was; knowledge of how men behaved and how they could be persuaded to do something if one approached the matter in the right way. She had told the apprentice no lies; there were girls who would be impressed by a young man who did a parachute jump and who had his photograph in the papers. If men were prepared to use psychology, which they usually were not, then they too could get women to do what they wanted them to do. Perhaps it was fortunate, then, that men were so bad at psychology. Men got women to do what they wanted through making them feel sorry for them, or making them feel guilty. Men did not do this deliberately, of course, but that was the effect.

The apprentice leaned out of his window and shouted at the donkeys, who looked at him balefully before they began to move slowly out of the way. Then, sitting back in his seat, he turned to Mma Ramotswe. "I think I will do it, Mma. I think that maybe it is a good idea to help the orphan farm. We should all do that we can."

WHEN MMA RAMOTSWE returned to Zebra Drive it was already beginning to get dark. Mr J.L.B. Matekoni's truck was parked at the side of the house, in the special spot that she had set aside for him, and she tucked the tiny white van into its own place near the kitchen door. Lights were on in the house, and she heard the sound of voices. They would be wondering, she thought, where she was, and they would be hungry.

She went into the kitchen, kicking off her shoes as she entered. Motholeli was in her wheelchair, behind the kitchen table, chopping carrots, and Puso was stirring something on the stove. Mr J.L.B. Matekoni, standing just behind the boy, was dropping a pinch of salt into the mixture in the pot.

"We are cooking your dinner tonight," said Mr J.L.B. Matekoni. "You can go and sit down, with your feet on a stool. We will call you when everything is ready."

Mma Ramotswe gave a cry of delight. "That is a very big treat for me," she said. "I am very tired for some reason."

She went through to the sitting room and dropped into her favourite chair. Although the children helped in the kitchen, it was unusual for them to cook a full meal. It must have been Mr J.L.B. Matekoni's idea, she reflected, and the thought filled her with gratitude that she had such a man who would think to cook a meal. Most husbands would never do that—would regard it as beneath their dignity to work in the house—but Mr J.L.B. Matekoni was different. It was as if he knew what it was like to be a woman, to have all that cooking to do, for the rest of one's life, a whole procession of pots and pans stretching out into the distance, seemingly endless. Women knew all about that, and dreamed about cooking and pots and the like, but here was a man who seemed to understand.

When they sat down to table half an hour later, Mma Ramotswe watched proudly as Mr J.L.B. Matekoni and Puso brought in the plates of good rich food and set them at each place. Then she said grace, as she always did, her eyes lowered to the tablecloth, as was proper.

"May the Lord look down kindly on Botswana," said Mma

Ramotswe. "And now we thank Him for the food on our plates which has been cooked so well." She paused. There was more to be said about that, but for the time being she felt that what she had said was enough and since everybody was very hungry they should all begin.

"This is very good," she said after the first mouthful. "I am very happy that I have such good cooks right here in my own house."

"It was Mr J.L.B. Matekoni's idea," said Motholeli. "Maybe he could start a Tlokweng Road Speedy Restaurant."

Mr J.L.B. Matekoni laughed. "I could not do that. I am only good at fixing cars. That is all I can do."

"But you can jump by parachute," said Motholeli. "You can do that too. They were talking about it at school."

There was a sudden silence, and it seemed as if a cloud had passed over the gathering. Mr J.L.B. Matekoni's fork paused where it was, half way to his mouth, and Mma Ramotswe's knife stopped cutting into a large piece of pumpkin. She looked up at Mr J.L.B. Matekoni, who held her glance only for a moment before he looked away.

"Oh that," said Mma Ramotswe. "That is all a mistake. Mr J.L.B. Matekoni was going to do a parachute jump, but now Charlie, the apprentice at the garage, has offered to do it instead. I have already spoken to Mma Potokwane about it and she is very pleased with the new arrangements. She said that she was sure that Mr J.L.B. Matekoni would want to give that young man a chance, and I said I would ask him what he thought."

They all looked at Mr J.L.B. Matekoni, whose eyes had opened wide as Mma Ramotswe spoke.

"Well?" said Mma Ramotswe, returning to her task of cutting the pumpkin. "What would you like to do, Mr J.L.B. Matekoni? Would you like to give that boy a chance?"

Mr J.L.B. Matekoni looked up at the ceiling. "I could do, I suppose," he said.

"Good," said Mma Ramotswe. "You are a very generous man. Charlie will be very pleased."

Mr J.L.B. Matekoni smiled. "It is nothing," he said. "Nothing."

They continued with the meal. Mma Ramotswe noticed that Mr J.L.B. Matekoni appeared to be in a very good mood and made several amusing remarks about the day's events, including a joke about a gearbox, which they all laughed at but which none of them understood. Then, when the plates were cleared away and the children were out of the room, Mr J.L.B. Matekoni left his chair and, standing over Mma Ramotswe's chair, he took her hand and said, "You are a kind woman, Mma Ramotswe, and I am very lucky to have found a lady like you. My life is a very happy one now."

"And I am happy too," said Mma Ramotswe. She was not going to be a widow after all, and she had managed to make it seem as if it had been his decision. That was what men liked—she was sure of it—and why should men not be allowed to think that they were getting what they liked, occasionally at least? She saw no reason why not.

CHAPTER TEN

MR J.L.B. MATEKONI'S DREAM

MR J.L.B. Matekoni was, of course, immensely relieved that Mma Ramotswe had presented him with the opportunity to withdraw from the parachute jump. She had done it so graciously, and so cleverly, that he had been saved all embarrassment. Throughout that day he had been plagued by anxiety as he reflected on the position in which Mma Potokwane had placed him. He was not a cowardly man, but he had felt nothing but fear, sheer naked fear, when he thought about the parachute jump. Eventually, by mid-afternoon, he had reached the conclusion that this was going to be the way in which he would die, and he had spent almost an hour thinking about the terms of a will which he would draw up the following day. Mma Ramotswe would get the garage, naturally, and she could run it with Mma Makutsi, who could become Manager again. His house would be sold—it would get a very good price—and the money could then be distributed amongst his cousins, who were not well-off and who would be able to use it to buy cattle. Mma Ramotswe should keep some of it, perhaps as much as half, as this would help to keep the children, who were his responsibility after all. And then there was his truck, which could go to the orphan farm, where a good use would be found for it.

At this point he stopped. Leaving the truck to the orphan farm was tantamount to leaving it to Mma Potokwane, and he was not at all sure whether this was what he wanted. It was Mma Potokwane, after all, who had caused this crisis in the first place and he saw no reason why she should profit from it. In one view of the matter, Mma Potokwane would be responsible for his death, and perhaps she should even be put on trial. That would teach her to push people around as she did. That would be a lesson to all powerful matrons, and he suspected that there were many such women. Men would simply have to fight back, and this could be done, on their behalf, by the Attorney-General of Botswana himself, who could start a show trial of Mma Potokwane—for homicide—for the sake of all men. That would at least be a start.

Such unworthy thoughts were now no longer necessary, and after that glorious release pronounced by Mma Ramotswe at the dinner table, Mr J.L.B. Matekoni felt no need to plan his will. That night, after he had returned to his house near the old Botswana Defence Force Club, he contemplated his familiar possessions, not with the eye of one who was planning their testamentary disposal, but with the relief of one who knew that he was not soon to be separated from them. He looked at his sofa, with its stained arms and cushions, and thought about the long Saturday afternoons that he had spent just sitting there, listening to the radio and thinking about nothing in particular. Then he looked at the velvet picture of a mountain that hung on the wall opposite the sofa. That was a fine picture which must have taken the artist a great deal of time to make. Mr J.L.B. Matekoni knew every detail of it. All of this would go over to Mma Ramotswe's house one of these days, but for the time being it was reassuring to see things so firmly and predictably in their proper place.

It was almost midnight by the time Mr J.L.B. Matekoni went to bed. He read the paper for a few minutes before he put out the light, drowsily dropping the paper by his bedside, and then, enveloped in darkness, he drifted into the sleep that had always come so easily to him after a day of hard work. Sleep was welcome; the nightmare that he had experienced had been a diurnal one, and now it was resolved. There was to be no drop, no plummet to the ground, no humiliation as his fear made itself manifest to all . . .

That was in the waking world; the sleeping world of Mr J.L.B. Matekoni had not caught up with the events of that evening, with the release from his torment, and at some point that night, he found himself standing on the edge of the tarmac at the airport, with a small white plane of the sort used by the Kalahari Flying Club taxi-ing towards him. A door of the plane was opened, and he was beckoned within by the pilot, who, as it happened, was Mma Potokwane herself.

"Get in, Mr J.L.B. Matekoni," shouted Mma Potokwane above the noise of the engine. She seemed vaguely annoyed that he was holding things up in some way, and Mr J.L.B. Matekoni obeyed, as he always did.

Mma Potokwane seemed quite confident, leaning forward to flick switches and adjust instruments. Mr J.L.B. Matekoni reached to touch a switch that appeared to need attention, as an orange light was flashing behind it, but his hand was brushed away by Mma Potokwane.

"Don't touch!" she shouted, as if addressing an orphan. "Dangerous!"

He sat back, and the little plane shot forward down the runway. The trees were so close, he thought, the grass so soft that he could jump out now, roll over, and escape; but there was no getting away from Mma Potokwane, who looked at him crossly and shook a finger in admonition. And then they were airborne, and he looked out of the window of the plane at the land below him, which was growing smaller and smaller, a miniaturised Botswana of cattle like ants and roads like thin strips of twisting brown thread. Oh, it was so beautiful to look down on his land and see the clouds and the blue and all the air. One might so easily step out onto such clouds and drift away, off to the West, over the great brown, and alight somewhere where the lions walked and where there were springs of water and tall trees and little sign of man.

Mma Potokwane pulled on the controls of the plane and they circled, hugging the edge of the town so far below. He looked down and he saw Zebra Drive; it was so easy to spot it, and was that not Mma Ramotswe waving to him from her yard, and Mma Makutsi, in her new green shoes? They were waving, smiling up at him, pointing to a place on the ground where he might land. He turned to Mma Potokwane, who smiled at him now and pointed to the handle of the door.

He reached out and no more than touched the door before it flew open. He felt the wind on his face, and the panic rose in him, and he tried to stop himself falling, holding onto one of the levers in the plane, a little thing that gave him no purchase. Mma Potokwane was shouting at him, taking her hands off the controls of the plane to shove him out, and now kicked him firmly in the back with those flat brown shoes which she wore to walk about the orphan farm. "Out!" she cried, and Mr J.L.B. Matekoni, mute with fear, slipped out into the empty air and tumbled, head over heels, now looking at the sky, now at the ground, down to the earth that was still so far away beneath him.

There was no parachute, of course, just pyjamas, and they were billowing about him, hardly slowing him up at all. *This is how it ends*, thought Mr J.L.B. Matekoni, and he began to think of how good life had been, and how precious; but he could not think of these things for long, for his fall was over in seconds and he landed on his feet, perfectly, as if he might have hopped off an old orange box at the garage; and there he was, out in the bush, beside a termite mound. He looked about him; it was an unfamiliar landscape, perhaps Tlokweng, perhaps not, and he was studying it when he heard his father's voice behind him. He turned round, but there was no sign of his father, who was there but not quite there, in the way in which the dead can come to us in our dreams. There was much that he wanted to ask his father, there was much that he wanted to tell him about the garage, but his father spoke first, in a voice which was strange and reedy—for a dead man has no breath to make a voice—and asked a question which woke up Mr J.L.B. Matekoni, wrenching him from his dream with its satisfactory soft landing by the termite mound.

"When are you going to marry Mma Ramotswe?" asked his father. "Isn't it about time?"

CHAPTER ELEVEN

MEETING MR BOBOLOGO

MMA RAMOTSWE had not been ignoring Mma Holonga's case. It was true that she had as yet done nothing, but that did not mean that she had not been thinking about how she would approach this delicate issue. It would not do for any of the men to discover that they were being investigated, as this would give offence and could easily drive away any genuine suitor. This meant that she would have to make enquiries with discretion, talking to people who knew these men and, if at all possible, engineering a meeting with them herself. That would require a pretext, but she was confident that one could be found.

The first thing she would have to do, she thought, was to talk to somebody who worked at Mr Bobologo's school. This was not difficult, as Mma Ramotswe's maid, Rose, had a cousin who had for many years been in charge of the school kitchen. She had stopped working now, and was living in Old Naledi, where she looked after the children of one of her sons. Mma Ramotswe had never met her, but Rose had mentioned her from time to time and assured her employer that a visit would be welcome.

"She is one of these people who is always talking," said Rose.

"She talks all day, even if nobody listens to her. She will be very happy to talk to you."

"Such people are very helpful in our work," said Mma Ramotswe. "They tell us things we need to know."

"This is such a lady," said Rose. "She will tell you everything she knows. It makes her very happy to do that. You will need a long, long time."

There were many people like that in Botswana, Mma Ramotswe reflected, and she was glad that this was so. It would be strange to live in a country where people were silent, passing one another in the street wordlessly, as if frightened of what the other might think or say. This was not the African way, where people would call out and converse with one another from opposite sides of a road, or across a wide expanse of bush, careless of who heard. Such conversations could be carried on by people walking in different directions, until voices grew too faint and too distant to be properly heard and words were swallowed by the sky. That was a good way of parting from a friend, so less abrupt than words of farewell followed by silence. Mma Ramotswe herself often shouted out to the children after they had left the house for school, reminding Puso to be careful of how he crossed the road or telling him to make sure that his shoelaces were tied properly, not that boys ever bothered about that sort of thing. Nor did boys ensure that their shirts were tucked into their trousers properly, but that was another issue which she could think about later, when the demands of clients were less pressing.

Rose's cousin, Mma Seeonyana, was at home when Mma Ramotswe called on her. Her house was not a large one—no more than two small rooms, Mma Ramotswe saw—but her yard was scrupulously clean, with circles traced in the sand by her wide-headed broom. This was a good sign; an untidy yard was a

sign of a woman who no longer bothered with the traditional
Botswana virtues, and such people, Mma Ramotswe found, were
almost always unreliable or rude. They had no idea of *botho,*
which meant respect or good manners. *Botho* set Botswana apart
from other places; it was what made it a special place. There
were people who mocked it, of course, but what precisely did
they want instead? Did they want people to be selfish? Did they
want them to treat others unkindly? Because if you forgot about
botho, then that was surely what would happen; Mma Ramotswe
was sure of that.

She saw Mma Seeonyana standing outside her front door, a
brown paper bag in her hand. As she parked the tiny white van at
the edge of the road, she noticed the older woman watching her.
This was another good sign. It was a traditional Botswana pursuit
to watch other people and wonder what they were up to; this
modern habit of indifference to others was very hard to understand. If you watched people, then it was a sign that you cared
about them, that you were not treating them as complete
strangers. Again, it was all a question of manners.

Mma Ramotswe stood at the gate and called out to Mma
Seeonyana. The other woman responded immediately, and
warmly, inviting Mma Ramotswe to come in and sit with her at
the back of the house, where it was shadier. She did not ask her
visitor what she wanted, but welcomed her, as if she were a friend
or neighbour who had called in for a chat.

"You are the woman who lives over that way, on Zebra Drive,"
said Mma Seeonyana. "You are the woman who employs Rose.
She has told me about you."

Mma Ramotswe was surprised that she had been recognised,
but further explanation was quickly provided. "Your van is very
well-known," said Mma Seeonyana. "Rose told me about it, and I
have seen you driving through town. I have often thought: I

would like to get to know that lady, but I never thought I would have the chance. I am very happy to see you here, Mma."

"I have heard of you too," said Mma Ramotswe. "Rose has spoken very well of you. She was very proud that you were in charge of those school kitchens."

Mma Seeonyana laughed. "When I was in that place I was feeding four hundred children every day," she said. "Now I am feeding two little boys. It is much easier."

"That is what we women must do all the time," said Mma Ramotswe. "I am feeding three people now. I have a fiancé and I have two children who are adopted and who come from the orphan farm. I have to make many meals. It seems that women have been put in the world to cook and keep the yard tidy. Sometimes I think that is very unfair and must be changed."

Mma Seeonyana agreed with this view of the world, but frowned when she thought of the implications. "The trouble is that men would never be able to do what we do," she said. "Most men will just not cook. They are too lazy. They would rather go hungry than cook. That is a big problem for us women. If we started to do other things, then the men would fade away and die of hunger. That is the problem."

"We could train them," said Mma Ramotswe. "There is much to be said for training men."

"But you have to find a man to train," said Mma Seeonyana. "And they just run away if you try to tell them what to do. I have had three men run away from me. They said that I talked too much and that they had no peace. But that is not true."

Mma Ramotswe clicked her tongue in sympathy. "No, Mma, it cannot be true. But sometimes men seem not to like us to talk to them. They think they have already heard what we have to say."

Mma Seeonyana sighed. "They are very foolish."

"Yes," said Mma Ramotswe. Some men were foolish, she

thought, but by no means all. And there were some very foolish women too, if one thought about it.

"Even teachers," said Mma Seeonyana. "Even teachers can be foolish sometimes."

Mma Ramotswe looked up sharply. "You must have known many teachers, Mma," she said. "When you were working in that place you must have known all the teachers."

"Oh I did," said Mma Seeonyana. "I knew many teachers. I saw them come as junior teachers and I saw them get promotion and become senior teachers. I saw all that happening. And I saw some very bad teachers too."

Mma Ramotswe affected surprise. "Bad teachers, Mma? Surely not."

"Oh yes," said Mma Seeonyana. "I was astonished over what I found out. But I suppose teachers are the same as anybody else and they can be bad sometimes."

Mma Ramotswe looked down at the ground. "Who were these bad teachers?" she asked. "And why were they bad?"

Mma Seeonyana shook her head. "They came and went," she said. "I do not remember all their names. But I do remember a man who came to the school for six months and then the police took him away. They said he had done a very bad thing, but they never told us what it was."

Mma Ramotswe shook her head. "That must have been very bad." She paused, and then, "The good teachers must have been ashamed. Teachers like Mr Bobologo, for example. He's a good teacher, isn't he?"

She had not expected the reply, which was a peal of laughter. "Oh that one! Yes, Mma. He's very good all right."

Mma Ramotswe waited for something more to be said, but Mma Seeonyana merely smiled, as if she were recalling some private, amusing memory. She would have to winkle this out without giving the impression of being too interested. "Oh," she said. "So he's a ladies' man, is he? I might have suspected it. There are so many ladies' men these days. I am surprised that there are any ordinary husbands left at all."

This brought forth another burst of laughter from Mma Seeonyana, who wiped at her eyes with the cuff of her blouse. "A ladies' man, Mma? Yes, I suppose you could say that! A ladies' man! Yes. Mr Bobologo would be very pleased to hear that, Mma."

Mma Ramotswe felt a momentary irritation with Mma Seeonyana. It was discourteous, in her view, to make vague allusions in one's conversation with another—allusions which the other could not understand. There was nothing more frustrating than trying to work out what another person was saying in the face of coyness or even deliberate obfuscation. If there was something which Mma Seeonyana wanted to say about Mr Bobologo, then she should say it directly rather than hinting at some private knowledge.

"Well, Mma," said Mma Ramotswe in a firm tone. "Is Mr Bobologo a ladies' man, or is he not?"

Mma Seeonyana stared at her. She was still smiling, but she had picked up the note of irritation in her visitor's voice and the smile was fading. "I'm sorry, Mma," she said. "I didn't mean to laugh like that. It's just that . . . well, it's just that you touched upon a very funny thing with that man. He is a ladies' man, but only in a very special sense. That was what was so funny."

Mma Ramotswe nodded encouragingly. "In what sense is he a ladies' man then?"

Mma Seeonyana chuckled. "He is one of those men who is worried about street ladies. These bad girls who hang about in bars. That sort of woman. He disapproves of them very strongly and he and some friends of his have been trying for years to save these girls from their bad ways. It is his hobby. He goes to the bus station and hands leaflets to young girls coming in from the villages. He warns them about what can happen in Gaborone."

Mma Ramotswe narrowed her eyes. This was very interesting information, but it was difficult to see what exactly it told her. Everybody was aware of the problem of bar girls, who were the scourge of Africa. It was sad to see them, dressed in their shoddy finery, flirting with older men who should know better, but who almost inevitably did not. Nobody liked this, but most people did nothing about it. At least Mr Bobologo and his friends were trying.

"It's a hopeless task," Mma Seeonyana continued. "They have set up some sort of place where these girls can go and live while they try to get honest jobs. It is over there by the African Mall." She stopped and looked at Mma Ramotswe. "But I'm sure that you didn't come here to talk about Mr Bobologo, Mma. There are better things to talk about."

Mma Ramotswe smiled. "I have been very happy to talk about him," she replied. "But if there are other things you would like to talk about, I am happy with that."

Mma Seeonyana sighed. "There are so many things to talk about, Mma. I don't really know where to start."

This, thought Mma Ramotswe, was a good cue, and she took it. She remembered Rose's warning, and she could see the afternoon, her precious Sunday afternoon, disappearing before her. "Well, I could always come back to visit you, Mma . . ."

"No," said Mma Seeonyana quickly. "You must stay, Mma. I will make you some tea and then I can tell you about something that has been happening around here that is very strange."

"You are very kind, Mma."

Mma Ramotswe sat down on the battered chair which Mma Seeonyana had pulled out of the doorway. This was duty, she supposed, and there were more uncomfortable ways of earning a living than listening to ladies like Mma Seeonyana gossiping about neighbourhood affairs. And one never knew what one might learn from such conversations. It was her duty to keep herself informed, as one could not tell when some snippet of information gathered in such a way would prove useful; just as the information about Mr Bobologo and the bar girls might prove useful, or might not. It was difficult to tell.

MMA MAKUTSI was also busy that Sunday, not on the affairs of the No. 1 Ladies' Detective Agency, but on the move to her new house. The simplest way of doing this would have been to ask Mma Ramotswe to bring her tiny white van to carry over her possessions, but she was unwilling to impose in this way. Mma Ramotswe was generous with her time, and would have readily agreed to help her, but Mma Makutsi was independent and decided to hire a truck and a driver for the hour or so it would take to move her effects to their new home. There was not much to move, after all: her bed, with its thin coir mattress which she would soon replace, her single chair, her black tin trunk with her clothes folded within it, and a box containing her shoes, her pot, pan, and small primus stove. These were the worldly goods of Mma Makutsi which were quickly piled up in the back of the truck by the muscular young man who drove up the bumpy track that morning.

"You have packed this well," he said, making conversation as they drove the short distance to her new house. "I move things for people all the time. But they often have many boxes and plastic bags full of things. Sometimes they also have a grandmother to be moved, and I have to put the old lady in the back of the truck with all the other things."

"That is no way to treat a grandmother," said Mma Makutsi. "The grandmother should ride in the front."

"I agree, Mma," said the young man. "Those people who put their grandmother in the back of the truck, they will feel sorry when the grandmother is late. They will remember that they put her in the back of the truck, and it will be too late to do anything about it."

Mma Makutsi replied to this observation civilly, and the rest of the journey was completed in silence. She had the key of the house in the pocket of her blouse and she felt for it from time to time just to reassure herself that it was really there. She was thinking, too, of how she would arrange the furniture—such as it was—and how she might see about a rug for her new bedroom. That was a previously undreamed-of luxury; she had woken every day of her life to a packed earth floor or to plain concrete. Now she might afford a rug which would feel so soft underfoot, like a covering of new grass. She closed her eyes and thought of what lay ahead—the luxury of having her own shower—with hot water!—and the pleasure, the sheer pleasure, of having an extra room in which she could entertain people if she wished. She could invite friends to have a meal with her, and nobody would have to sit on a bed or look at her tin trunk. She could buy a radio and they could listen to music together, Mma Makutsi and her friends, and they would talk about important things, and all the humiliations of the shared stand-pipe would be a thing of the past.

She kept her eyes closed until they were almost there and then opened them and saw the house, which seemed smaller now than she had remembered it, but which was still so beautiful in her eyes, with its sloping roof and its paw-paw trees.

"This is your place, Mma?" asked the driver.

"It's my house," said Mma Makutsi, savouring the words.

"You're lucky," said the young man. "This is a good place to live. How many pula is the rent? What do you pay?"

Mma Makutsi told him and he whistled. "That is a lot! I

could not afford a place like this. I have to live in half a room over that way, half way to Molepolole."

"That cannot be easy," said Mma Makutsi.

They drew up in front of the gate, and Mma Makutsi walked down the short path that led to the front door. She had that door, and the part of the house which was lived in by the other tenants was reached by the door at the back. She felt proud that the front door was hers, even if it looked as if it was in need of a coat of paint. That could be dealt with later; what counted now was that she had the key to this door in her hand, paid for by the first month's rent, and hers by right.

It took the young man very little time to move her possessions into the front room. She thanked him, and gave him a ten-pula tip—overly generous, perhaps, but she was a proper householder now and these things would be expected of her. As she handed over the money, which he took from her with a wide smile, she reflected on the fact that she had never done this before. She had never before been in a position where she had given largesse, and the thought struck her forcibly. It was an unfamiliar, slightly uncomfortable feeling; I am just Mma Makutsi, from Bobonong, and I am giving this young man a ten-pula note. I have more money than he has. I have a better house. I am where he would like to be, but isn't.

By herself now, in the house, Mma Makutsi moved about her two rooms. She touched the walls; they were solid. She loosened a window latch, letting in a warm breeze for a moment, and then closed the window again. She switched on a light, and a bulb glowed above her; she turned on a tap, and water, fresh, cold water came out and splashed into a stainless steel sink, so polished and shiny that she could see her face reflected at her, the face of a person who was looking at the world with the cautious wonder of ownership, or at least of something close to it, of tenancy.

There was a side door to the house, and she opened this and peered out onto the yard. The paw-paw trees had incipient fruit upon them, which would be ready in a month or so. There were one or two other plants, shrubs that had wilted in the heat but which had the dogged determination of indigenous Botswana vegetation. These would survive even if never watered; they would cling on in the dry ground, making the most of what little moisture they could draw from the soil, tenacious because they lived here in this dry country, and had always lived here. Mma Ramotswe had once described the traditional plants of Botswana as loyal and yes, that was right, thought Mma Makutsi, that is what they are—our old friends, our fellow survivors in this brown land that I love and love so much. Not that she thought about that love very often, but it was there, as it was in the hearts of all Batswana. And that was surely what most people wanted, at the end of the day; to live on the land that they love, and nowhere else; to be where their people had been before them, as long as anybody could remember.

She drew back from the door, and looked about her house again. She did not see the grubby finger marks on the wall, nor the place where the floor had buckled. What she saw was a room with bright curtains and with friends about a table, and herself at the head; what she heard was a pot of water boiling on a stove, to the soft hissing of a flame.

CHAPTER TWELVE

MR BOBOLOGO TALKS ON THE SUBJECT
OF LOOSE WOMEN

THE FACT that the schools were on holiday was convenient. Had Mr Bobologo been teaching, then Mma Ramotswe would have been obliged to wait until half past three, when she could have accosted him on his way to the house that he occupied in the neat row of teachers' houses at the back of the school. As it was, that Monday she was able to arrive at his house at ten o'clock and find him, as Mma Seeonyana said she would, sitting on a chair in the sun outside his back door, a Bible on his lap. She approached him carefully, as one always should when coming across somebody reading the Bible, and greeted him in the approved, traditional fashion. Had he slept well? Was he well? Would he mind if she talked to him?

Mr Bobologo looked up at her, squinting against the sunlight, and Mma Ramotswe saw a tall man of slim build, carefully dressed in khaki trousers and an open-necked white shirt, and wearing a pair of round, pebble-lensed glasses. Everything about him, from the carefully polished brown shoes to the powerful glasses, said *teacher*, and she had to make an effort to prevent herself from smiling. People were so predictable, she thought, so true to type. Bank managers dressed exactly as bank managers were expected to dress—and behaved accordingly; you could always tell a lawyer from that careful, rather watchful way they listened to what you had to say, as if they were ready to pounce on the slightest slip; and, since she had come to know Mr J.L.B. Matekoni, there was no mistaking mechanics, who looked at things as if they were ready to take them apart and make them work better. Not that this applied to all mechanics, of course; the apprentices would be mechanics before too long and yet they looked at things as if they were about to break them. So perhaps it took years before a calling began to tell on a person.

Did she look like a detective, she wondered? This was an intriguing question. If somebody saw her in the street, they would probably not look twice at her. She was just an ordinary Motswana lady, in the traditional mould, going about her daily business as so many other women did. Surely nobody would suspect her of *watching*, which is what she had to do in her job. Perhaps it was different with Mma Makutsi, with those large glasses of hers. People noticed those glasses and clearly thought about them. They might wonder, might they not, why somebody would need such large glasses and they might conclude that this was because she was interested in looking closely at things, at magnifying them. That, of course, was an absurd vision of what she and Mma Makutsi did; they very rarely had to examine any physical objects—human behaviour was what interested them, and all that this required was observation and understanding.

Her observation of Mr Bobologo lasted only a few seconds. Now he stood up, closing the Bible with some regret, as one might close a riveting novel in which one had become immersed. Of course Mr Bobologo would know the end of the story—which was not a happy ending, if one thought about it carefully—but one might still be absorbed even in the completely familiar.

"I am sorry to disturb you," said Mma Ramotswe. "The school

holidays must be a good time for you teachers to catch up on your reading. You will not like people coming along and disturbing you."

Mr Bobologo responded well to this courteous beginning. "I am happy to see you, Mma. There will be plenty of time for reading later on. You may sit on this chair and I will fetch another."

Mma Ramotswe sat on the teacher's chair and waited for him to return. It was a good spot that he had chosen to sit, hidden from passers-by on the road, but with a view of the children's playground where even now in the holidays the children of the school staff were engaged in some complicated game with a ball. It would be good to sit here, she thought, knowing that the Government was still paying one's salary every month, and that reading, and becoming wiser and wiser, was exactly what one was expected to do.

Mr Bobologo returned with another chair and seated himself opposite Mma Ramotswe. He looked at her through the thick lenses of his spectacles, and then dabbed gently at the side of his mouth with a white handkerchief, which he then folded neatly and placed in the pocket of his shirt.

Mma Ramotswe looked back at him and smiled. Her initial impression of Mr Bobologo had been favourable, but she found herself wondering why it was that a successful, rather elegant person such as Mma Holonga should take up with this teacher, who, whatever his merits might be, was hardly a romantic figure. But such speculation was inevitably fruitless. The choices that people made in such circumstances were often inexplicable, and perhaps it was no more than sheer chance. If you were in the mood for falling in love, or marrying, then perhaps it did not matter very much whom you would see when you turned the corner. You were looking for somebody, and there was somebody, and you would convince yourself that this random person was what you were really looking for in the first place. *We find what we are looking for in life*, her father had once said to her; which was true—if you look for happiness, you will see it; if you look for distrust and envy and hatred—all those things—you will find those too.

"So, Mma," said Mr Bobologo. "Here I am. You have come to see me about your child, I assume. I hope I can say that this boy or this girl is doing well at school. I am sure I can. But first you must tell me what your name is, so I know which child it is that I am talking about. That is important."

For a few moments Mma Ramotswe was taken aback, but then she laughed. "Oh no, Rra. Do not worry. I am not some troublesome mother who has come to talk about her difficult child. I have come because I have heard of your other work."

Mr Bobologo took out his handkerchief and dabbed again at the side of his mouth.

"I see," he said. "You have heard of this work that I do." There was a note of suspicion in his voice, Mma Ramotswe noticed, and she wondered why this should be. Perhaps he was laughed at by others, or labelled a prude, and the thought irritated her. There was nothing to be ashamed of in the work that he did, even if it seemed strange for a man to have such strong views on such a matter. At least he was trying to help address a social problem, which was more than most people did.

"I have heard of it," said Mma Ramotswe. "And I thought that I would like to hear more about it. It is a good thing that you are doing, Rra."

Mr Bobologo's expression remained impassive. Mma Ramotswe thought that he was still unconvinced by what she had said, and so she continued, "The problem of these street girls is a very big one, Rra. Every time I see them going into bars, I think: *That girl is somebody's daughter*, and that makes me sad. That is what I think, Rra."

These words had a marked effect on Mr Bobologo. While she

was still speaking, he sat up in his chair, sharply, and stared intensely at Mma Ramotswe.

"You are right, Mma," he said. "They are all the daughters of some poor person. They are all children who have been loved by their parents, and by God himself, and now where are they? In bars! That is where. Or in the arms of some man. That is also where." He paused, looking down at the ground. "I am sorry to use such strong language, Mma. I am not a man who uses strong language, but when it comes to this matter, then I am like a dog who has been kicked in the ribs."

Mma Ramotswe nodded. "It is something that should make us all angry."

"Yes," said Mr Bobologo. "It should. It should. But what does the Government do about this? Do you see the Government going down to these bars and chasing these bad girls back to their villages? Do you see that, Mma?"

Mma Ramotswe mused for a moment. There were many things, she thought, that one could reasonably expect the Government to do, but it had never occurred to her that chasing bar girls back to their villages was one of them. For a moment she imagined the Minister of Roads, for example, a portly man who inevitably wore a wide-brimmed hat to shade him from the sun, chasing bar girls down the road to Lobatse, followed, perhaps, by his Under-Secretary and several clerks from the Ministry. It was an intriguing picture, and one which would normally have made her smile, but there was no question of smiling now, in front of the righteous indignation of Mr Bobologo.

"So I decided—together with some friends," continued Mr Bobologo, "that we should do something ourselves. And that is how we started the House of Hope."

Mma Ramotswe listened politely as Mr Bobologo listed the

difficulties he had encountered in finding a suitable building for the House of Hope and how eventually they had obtained a ruinously expensive lease on a house near the African Mall. It had three bedrooms and a living room which was not enough, he explained, for the fourteen girls who lived there. "Sometimes we have even had as many as twenty bad girls in that place," he said. "Twenty girls, Mma! All under one roof. When it is that full, then there is not enough room for anybody to do anything. They must sleep on the floor and doubled-up in bunks. That is not a good thing, because when things get that crowded they run away and we have to look for them again and persuade them to come back. It is very trying."

Mma Ramotswe was intrigued. If the girls ran away, then it implied that they were kept there against their will, which surely could not be the case. You could keep children in one place against their will, but you could not do that to bar girls, if they were over eighteen. There were obviously details of the House of Hope which would require further investigation.

"Would you show me this place, Rra?" she asked. "I can drive you down there in my van if you would show me. Then I will be able to understand the work that you are doing."

Mr Bobologo seemed to weigh this request for a moment, but then he rose to his feet, taking his glasses off and stowing them in his top pocket. "I am happy to do that, Mma. I am happy for people to see what we are doing so that they may tell other people about it. Perhaps they will even tell the Government and persuade them to give us money so that we can run the House of Hope on a proper basis. There is never ever enough money, and we have to rely on what we can get from churches and some generous people. The Government should pay for this, but do they help us? The answer to that, Mma, is no. The Government is not concerned about the welfare of ladies in this country. They think only of new roads and new buildings. That is what they think of."

"It is very unfair," agreed Mma Ramotswe. "I also have a list of things that I think the Government should do."

"Oh yes?" said Mr Bobologo. "And what is on your list, Mma?"

This question caught Mma Ramotswe by surprise. She had spoken of her list idly, as a conversational ploy; there was no list, really.

"So?" pressed Mr Bobologo. "So what is on this list of yours, Mma?"

Mma Ramotswe thought wildly. "I would like to see boys taught how to sew at school," she said. "That is on my list."

Mr Bobologo stared at her. "But that is not possible, Mma," he said dismissively. "That is not something that boys wish to learn. I am not surprised that the Government is not trying to teach boys this thing. You cannot teach boys to be girls. That is not good for boys."

"But boys wear clothes, do they not, Rra?" countered Mma Ramotswe. "And if these clothes are torn, then who is there to sew them up?"

"There are girls to do that," said Mr Bobologo. "There are girls and ladies. There are plenty of people in Botswana to do all the necessary sewing. That is a fact. I am a very experienced teacher and I know about these matters. Do you have anything else on your list, Mma?"

There would have been a time when Mma Ramotswe would not have allowed this to pass, but she was on duty now, and there was no need to antagonise Mr Bobologo. She owed it to her client to find out more about him, and that was a more immediate duty than her duty to the women of Botswana. So she merely looked up at the sky, as if looking for inspiration.

"I would like the Government to do many things," she said. "But I do not want to make them too tired. So I shall have to think about my list and make it a bit smaller."

Mr Bobologo looked at her approvingly. "I think that is very wise, Mma. If one asks for too many things at the same time, then one does not usually get them. If you ask for one thing, then you may get that one thing. That is what I have found in life."

"Ow!" exclaimed Mma Ramotswe. "You are a clever man, Rra!"

Mr Bobologo acknowledged the compliment with a brief nod of the head, and then indicated that he was now ready to follow Mma Ramotswe to the van. She stood aside and invited him to precede her, as was proper when dealing with a teacher. Whatever Mr Bobologo might prove to be like, he was first and foremost a teacher, and Mma Ramotswe believed very strongly that teachers should be treated with respect, as they always had been before the old Botswana morality had started to unravel. Now people treated teachers like anybody else, which was a grave mistake; no wonder children were so cheeky and ill-behaved. A society that undermined its teachers and their authority only dug away at its own sure foundations. Mma Ramotswe thought this was obvious; the astonishing thing was that many people simply did not understand that this was the case. But there was a great deal that people did not understand and would only learn through bitter experience. In her view, one of these things was the truth of the old African saying that it takes an entire village to raise a child. Of course it does; of course it does. Everybody in a village had a role to play in bringing up a child—and cherishing it—and in return that child would in due course feel responsible for everybody in that village. That is what makes life in society possible. We must love one another and help one another in our daily lives. That was the traditional African way and there was no substitute for it. None.

IT WAS only a few minutes' drive from the teachers' quarters to the House of Hope, a drive during which Mr Bobologo held on firmly to the side of the passenger seat, as if fearing that any moment Mma Ramotswe would steer the tiny white van off the road. Mma Ramotswe noticed this, but said nothing; there were some men who would never be happy with women drivers, even although the statistics were plain for them to see. Women had fewer accidents because they drove more sedately and were not trying to prove anything to anybody. It was men who were the reckless drivers—particularly young men (such as the apprentices) who felt that girls would be more impressed by speed than by safety. And it was young men in red cars who were the most dangerous of all. Such people were best given a wide berth, both in and out of the car.

"That is the House of Hope," said Mr Bobologo. "You can park under the tree here. Carefully, Mma. You do not wish to hit the tree. Careful!"

"I have never hit a tree in my life," retorted Mma Ramotswe. "But I have known many men who have hit trees, Rra. Some of those men are late now."

"It may not have been their fault," muttered Mr Bobologo.

"Yes," said Mma Ramotswe evenly. "It could have been the fault of the trees. That is always possible."

She was incensed by his remark and struggled to contain her anger. Unfortunately, her battle with her righteous indignation overcame her judgment, and she hit the tree; not hard, but with enough of a jolt to make Mr Bobologo grab onto his seat once again.

"There," he said, turning to her in triumph. "You have hit the tree, Mma."

Mma Ramotswe turned off the engine and closed her eyes. Clovis Andersen, author of her professional vade mecum, *The Principles of Private Detection,* had advice which was appropriate to this occasion, and Mma Ramotswe now called it to mind. *Never allow your personal feelings to cloud the issue,* he had written. *You may be seething with anger over something, but do not— and I repeat not—do not allow it to overcome your professional judgment. Keep your calm. That is the most important thing. And if you find it difficult, close your eyes and count to ten.*

By the time she reached ten, Mr Bobologo had opened his door and was waiting for her outside. So Mma Ramotswe swallowed hard and joined him, following him up the short garden path that led to the doorway of an unexceptional white-washed house, of much the same sort as could be seen on any nearby street, and which from the road would never have been identified—without special knowledge—as a house of hope, or indeed of despair, or of anything else for that matter. It was just a house, and yet here it was, filled to the brim with bad girls.

"Here we are, Mma," said Mr Bobologo as he approached the front door. "Take up hope all you who enter here. That is what we say, and one day we shall have it written above the door."

Mma Ramotswe looked at the unprepossessing door. Her reservations about Mr Bobologo were growing, but she was not quite sure why this should be so. He was irritating, of course, but so were many people, and being irritating was not enough for him to be written off. No, there was something more than that. Was it smugness, or singularity of purpose? Perhaps that was it. It was always disconcerting to meet those who had become so obsessed with a single topic that they could not see their concerns in context. Such people were uncomfortable company purely because they lacked normal human balance, and this, she thought, might be the case with Mr Bobologo. And yet she had not been asked to find out whether Mr Bobologo was an interesting man, or even a nice man. She had been asked to find out whether he was after Mma Holonga's money. That was a very specific question, and her feelings for Mr Bobologo had nothing to do with the answer to that question. So she would give him the benefit of the doubt, and keep her personal opinions to herself. She herself would never marry Mr Bobologo—or any man like him—but it would be wrong of her to interfere until she had very concrete proof of the exact issue at stake. And that had not yet appeared, and might never appear. So for the time being, the only thing to do was to concentrate on inspecting the House of Hope and wait until Mr Bobologo put a foot wrong and gave himself away. And she had a feeling now—a fairly strong feeling—that he might never do that.

CHAPTER THIRTEEN

MR J.L.B. MATEKONI RECEIVES THE BUTCHER'S CAR; THE APPRENTICES RECEIVE AN ANONYMOUS LETTER

WHILE MMA RAMOTSWE was visiting Mr Bobologo and his House of Hope, Mr J.L.B. Matekoni was completing a tricky repair at Tlokweng Road Speedy Motors. He was relieved, of course, about the cancellation of the parachute jump, but at the same time he was concerned about the fact that one of the apprentices was going to do it in his stead. He knew that these boys were feckless, and he knew that they would do anything to impress girls, but he was their apprentice-master, after all, and he considered that he had a moral responsibility for them until they had served out their apprenticeship. Many people would say that this did not extend to cover what they did in their own time, but Mr J.L.B. Matekoni was not one to take a narrow view of these matters and he could not avoid feeling at least slightly paternal towards these young men, irritating though they undoubtedly were. He was not sure, though, how he could deal with this issue. If he persuaded the young man not to jump, then Mma Potokwane might insist that he do the jump after all. If she did so, then that would lead to a row between her and Mma Ramotswe, and that could become complicated. There might be no more fruit cake, for example, and he would miss his trips out to see the orphans, even if he was inevitably given some task to perform the moment he arrived at the orphan farm.

The repair took less time than he had anticipated, and well before it was time for the morning break Mr J.L.B. Matekoni found himself wiping the steering wheel and the driver's seat to make the car ready for collection by its owner. He was always very careful to ensure that cars were returned to the customer in a clean state—something he had attempted to drill into the apprentices, but without success.

"How would you feel if your car came back to you with greasy fingerprints all over it?" he said to them. "Would you like it?"

"I would not see them," said one of the young men. "I am not worried about fingerprints. As long as a car goes fast, that is the only thing."

Mr J.L.B. Matekoni could barely credit what he had heard. "Do you mean to say that the only thing that advantages is speed? Is that what you really think?"

The apprentice had looked at him blankly before he gave his reply. "Of course. If a car goes fast, then it is a good car. It has a strong engine. Everybody knows that, Boss."

Mr J.L.B. Matekoni shook his head in despair. How many times had he explained about solid engineering and the merits of a reliable gearbox? How many times had he spelled out to these young men the merits of an economical engine, particularly a good diesel engine that would give years and years of service with very little trouble? Diesel-powered cars did not usually go very fast, but that was not the point; they were good cars anyway. None of these lessons, it appeared, had sunk in. He sighed. "I have been wasting my time," he muttered. "Wasting my time."

The apprentice smiled. "Wasting your time, Boss? What have you been doing? Dancing? You and Mma Ramotswe going dancing at one of those clubs? Hah!"

Mr J.L.B. Matekoni wanted to say, "Trying to teach a hyena to dance," but did not. Where had he heard that expression before? It seemed familiar, and then he remembered he had said it himself only a few days ago when he had been discussing First Class Motors with Mma Ramotswe. The memory made him start, and put the apprentices quite out of his mind. There was something hanging over him; he had forgotten what it was, but now it came back: he still had to deal with the issue of the butcher's car, which was due to be brought into the garage that morning. The thought appalled him: he would be able to effect a temporary repair, until such time as he tracked down the right parts, but there was more to it than that. He had agreed that he would confront the Manager of First Class Motors and tell him that his wrongdoing had been discovered. He did not relish this, in view of the other man's reputation. Indeed, it might have been moderately more attractive to do a parachute jump, perhaps, rather than meet the Manager of First Class Motors.

"You look worried," said the apprentice. "Is there something troubling you, Boss?"

Mr J.L.B. Matekoni sighed. "I have an unpleasant duty to do," he said. "I have to go and speak to some bad mechanics about their work. That is what is troubling me."

"Who are these bad mechanics?" asked the apprentice.

"Those people at First Class Motors," said Mr J.L.B. Matekoni. "The man who owns it and the men who work for him. They are all bad, every one of them."

The apprentice whistled. "Yes, they are bad all right. I have seen those people. They know nothing about cars. They are not like you, Mr J.L.B. Matekoni, who knows everything about all sorts of cars."

The compliment from the apprentice was unexpected, and

Mr J.L.B. Matekoni, in spite of his modesty, was touched by the young man's tribute.

"I am not a great mechanic," he said softly. "I am just careful, that is all, and that is what I have always wanted you to be. I would want you to be careful mechanics. It would make me very happy if you would be that."

"We will be," said the apprentice. "We will try to be like you. We hope that people will always look at our work and think: they learned that from Mr J.L.B. Matekoni."

Mr J.L.B. Matekoni smiled. "*Some* of your work, maybe . . ." he began, but the apprentice interrupted him.

"You see," he said, "my father is late. He became late when I was a small boy—just that high—very small. And I did not have uncles who were any good, and so I think of you as my father, Rra. That is what I think. You are my father."

Mr J.L.B. Matekoni was silent. He had always had difficulty in expressing his emotions—as mechanics often do, he thought—and it was hard for him now. He wanted to say to this young man: What you have said makes me very proud, and very sad, all at the same time—but he could not find these words. He could, however, place a hand on the young man's shoulder and leave it there for a moment, to show that he understood what had been said.

"I have never said thank you, Rra," went on the apprentice. "And I would not want you to die without being thanked by me."

Mr J.L.B. Matekoni gave a start. "Am I going to die?" he asked. "I am not all that old surely. I am still here."

The apprentice smiled. "I did not mean that you were going to die soon, Rra. But you will die one of these days, like everybody else. And I wanted to say thank you before that day came."

"Well," said Mr J.L.B. Matekoni, "what you say is probably true, but we have spent too much time standing here talking about these things. There is work to be done in the garage. We have to get rid of that dirty oil over there. You can take it over to the special dump for burning. You can take the spare truck."

"I will do that now," said the apprentice.

"And don't pick up any girls in the truck," warned Mr J.L.B. Matekoni. "You remember what I told you about the insurance."

The apprentice, who had been already walking away, suddenly stopped in his tracks, guiltily, and Mr J.L.B. Matekoni knew immediately that this was precisely what he had been planning to do. The young man had made a moving statement, and Mr J.L.B. Matekoni had been touched by what he had said, but some things obviously never changed.

A FEW HOURS later, as the sun climbed up the sky and made shadows short and even the birds were lethargic, when the screeching of the cicadas from the bush behind Tlokweng Road Speedy Motors had reached a high insistent pitch, the butcher drew up in his handsome old Rover. He had had the time to reflect on what Mr J.L.B. Matekoni had told him, and he now spoke angrily of First Class Motors, with whom he intended to have no further dealings. Only shame, the shame of being a victim, prevented him from returning there to ask for his money back.

"I shall do that for you, Rra," said Mr J.L.B. Matekoni. "I feel responsible for what my brother mechanics have done to you."

The butcher took Mr J.L.B. Matekoni's hand and shook it firmly. "You have been very good to me, Rra. I am glad that there are still some honest men left in Botswana."

"There are many honest men in Botswana," said Mr J.L.B. Matekoni. "I am no better than anybody else."

"Oh yes you are," said the butcher. "I see many men in my work and I can tell . . ."

Mr J.L.B. Matekoni cut him short. This was clearly a day for excessive compliments, and he was beginning to feel embarrassed. "You are very kind, Rra, but I must get on with my work. The flies will be settling on the cars if I don't look out."

He had spoken the words without thinking that a butcher might take such a remark as a slight, as a suggestion that his own meat was much beset by flies. But the butcher did not appear to mind, and he smiled at the metaphor. "There are flies everywhere," he said. "We butchers know all about that. I would like to find a country without flies. Is there such a place, do you think, Rra?"

"I have not heard of such a country," said Mr J.L.B. Matekoni. "I think that in very cold places there are no flies. Or in some very big towns, where there are no cattle to bring the flies. Perhaps in such places. Places like New York."

"Are there no cattle in New York?" asked the butcher.

"I do not think so," said Mr J.L.B. Matekoni.

The butcher thought for a moment. "But there is a big green part of the town. I have seen a photograph. This part, this bit of bush, is in the middle. Perhaps they keep the cattle there. Do you think that is the place for cattle, Rra?"

"Perhaps," said Mr J.L.B. Matekoni, glancing at his watch. It was time for him to go home for his lunch, which he always ate at noon. Then, after lunch, fortified by a plate of meat and beans, he would drive round to First Class Motors and speak to the Manager.

MMA MAKUTSI ate her own lunch in the office. Now that she had a bit more money from the Kalahari Typing School for Men, she was able to treat herself to a doughnut at lunchtime, and this she ate with relish, a magazine open on the desk before her, a cup of bush tea at her side. It was best, of course, if Mma Ramotswe was there too, as they could exchange news and opinions, but it was still enjoyable to be by oneself, turning the pages of the magazine with one hand and licking the sugar off the fingers of the other.

The magazine was a glossy one, published in Johannesburg, and sold in great numbers at the Botswana Book Centre. It contained articles about musicians and actors and the like, and about the parties which these people liked to attend in places like Cape Town and Durban. Mma Ramotswe had once said that she would not care to go to that sort of party, even if she were to be invited to one—which she never had been, as Mma Makutsi helpfully pointed out—but she was still sufficiently interested to peer over Mma Makutsi's shoulder and comment on the people in the pictures.

"That woman in the red dress," Mma Ramotswe had said. "Look at her. She is a lady who is only good for going to parties. That is very clear."

"She is a very famous lady, that one," Mma Makutsi had replied. "I have seen her picture many times. She knows where there are cameras and she stands in front of them, like a pig trying to get to the food. She is a very fashionable lady over in Johannesburg."

"And what is she famous for?"

"The magazine has never explained that," Mma Makutsi had said. "Maybe they do not know either."

This had made Mma Ramotswe laugh. "And then that woman there, that one in the middle, standing next to . . ." She had stopped, suddenly, as she recognised the face in the photograph. Mma Makutsi, engrossed in the contemplation of another photograph, had not noticed anything untoward. So she did not see the expression on Mma Ramotswe's face as she recognised, in the middle of the group of smiling friends, the face of Note Mokoti, trumpet player, and, for a brief and unhappy time, husband of Precious Ramotswe and father—not that it had meant anything to him—of her tiny child, the one who had left her after only those few, cherished hours.

Now, though, Mma Makutsi paged through the magazine on her own, while from within the garage there came the sound of a car's wheels being taken off. The sounds of wheel-nuts being thrown into an upturned hub-cap was one she recognised well, and was reassuring, in a strange way, just as the sound of the cicadas in the bush was a comforting one. The sounds that were alarming were those that came from nowhere, strange sounds that occurred at night, which might be anything.

She abandoned her magazine and reached for her tea cup, and it was at that point that she saw the envelope at the end of her desk. She had not noticed it when she came in that day, and it was not there last night, which meant that it must have been put there first thing in the morning. Mr J.L.B. Matekoni had opened the garage and the office, and he must have found it slipped under a door. Sometimes customers left notes that way, when they passed by and the garage was closed. Bills were even settled like this, with the money tucked into an envelope and pushed into the office through a crack in the door. That worried Mma Makutsi, who imagined that it would be very easy for money to go missing, but Mr J.L.B. Matekoni seemed unconcerned about it, and said that his customers had always paid in all sorts of ways and money had never been lost.

"One man used to pay his bills with bags of coins," he said. "Sometimes he would drive past, throw out one of those old white Standard Bank bags, wave, and drive off. That is how he settled his bills."

"That's all very well," Mma Makutsi had said. "But that would never have been recommended to us at the Botswana Secretarial College. They taught us there that the best way to pay bills was by cheque, and to ask for a receipt."

That was undoubtedly true, and Mr J.L.B. Matekoni had not cared to argue with one who had achieved the since then unequalled score of ninety-seven per cent in her final examinations at the Botswana Secretarial College. This letter, though, was plainly not a bill. As Mma Makutsi stretched across her desk to pick it up, she saw, written across the front of the envelope: *To Mr Handsome, Tlokweng Road Speedy Motors.*

She smiled. There was no means of telling who this Mr Handsome was—there were, after all, three men who worked at the garage and it could be addressed to any one of them—and this meant that she would be quite within her rights to open it.

There was a single sheet of paper inside the envelope, and Mma Makutsi unfolded this and began to read. *Dear Mr Handsome*, the letter began. *You do not know who I am, but I have been watching out for you! You are very handsome. You have a handsome face and handsome legs. Even your neck is handsome. I hope that you will talk to me one day. I am waiting for you. There is a lot we could talk about. Your admirer.*

Mma Makutsi finished reading and then folded the letter up and put it back in the envelope. People did send such notes to one another, she knew, but the senders usually made sure that the letters were picked up by those for whom they were intended. It was strange that this person, this admirer, whoever she was, should have put the letter under the door without giving any further clue as to which Mr Handsome she had in mind. Now it was up to her to decide who should get this letter. Mr J.L.B. Matekoni? No. He was not a handsome man; he was pleasant-looking in a comfortable sort of way, but he was not handsome, in that sense. And anyway, whoever it was who had left the letter had no business in sending a letter like that to an engaged man and she, Mma Makutsi, would most certainly never pass on a letter of this nature to Mr J.L.B. Matekoni, even if it had been intended for him.

It was much more likely, then, that the letter was intended for the apprentices. But which one? Charlie, the older apprentice, was certainly good-looking, in a cheap sort of way she thought, but the same could probably be said of the younger one, perhaps even more so, when one considered the amount of hair gel that he seemed to rub on his head. If one were a young woman, somebody aged perhaps seventeen or eighteen, it is easy to see how one would be taken in by the looks of these young men and how one might even write a letter of this sort. So there was really no way of telling which of the young men was the intended recipient. It might be simpler, then, to throw the letter in the bin, and Mma Makutsi had almost decided to do this when the older apprentice walked into the room. He saw the envelope on the desk before her and, with a typical lack of respect for what is right, peered at the writing on the envelope.

"To Mr Handsome," he exclaimed. "That letter must be for me!"

Mma Makutsi snorted. "You are not the only man around here. There are two others, you know. Mr J.L.B. Matekoni and that friend of yours, that one with the oil on his hair. It could be for either of them."

The apprentice stared at her uncomprehendingly. "But Mr J.L.B. Matekoni is at least forty," he said. "How can a man of forty be called Mr Handsome?"

"Forty is not the end," said Mma Makutsi. "People who are forty can look very good."

"To other people who are forty maybe," said the apprentice, "but not to the general public."

Mma Makutsi drew in her breath, and held it. If only Mma

Ramotswe had been here to listen to this; what would she have done? She certainly would not have let any of this pass. The effrontery of this young man! The sheer effrontery! Well, she would teach him a lesson, she would tell him what she thought of his vanity; she would spell it out . . . She stopped. A better idea had materialised; a wonderful trick that would amuse Mma Ramotswe when she told her about it.

"Call the young one in," she said. "Tell him I want to tell him about this letter you have received. He will be impressed, I think."

Charlie left and soon returned with the younger apprentice.

"Charlie here has received a letter," said Mma Makutsi. "It was addressed to Mr Handsome and I shall read it out to you."

The younger apprentice glanced at Charlie, and then looked back at Mma Makutsi. "But that could be for me," he said petulantly. "Why should he think that such a letter is addressed to him? What about me?"

"Or Mr J.L.B. Matekoni?" asked Mma Makutsi, smiling. "What about him?"

The younger apprentice shook his head. "He is an old man," he said. "Nobody would call him Mr Handsome. It is too late."

"I see," said Mma Makutsi. "Well, at least you are agreed on that. Well, let me read out the letter, and then we can decide."

She opened the envelope again, extracted the piece of paper, and read out the contents. Then, putting the letter down on the table, she smiled at the two young men. "Now who is being described in that letter? You tell me."

"Me," they both said together, and then looked at one another.

"It could be either," said Mma Makutsi. "Of course, I now remember who must have put that letter there. I have remembered something."

"You must tell me," said the older apprentice. "Then I can look out for this girl and talk to her."

"I see," said Mma Makutsi. She hesitated; this was a delicious moment. Oh, silly young men! "Yes," she continued, "I saw a man outside the garage this morning, first thing. Yes, there was a man."

There was complete silence. "A man?" said the younger apprentice eventually. "Not a girl?"

"It was for him, I think," said the older apprentice, gesturing at the younger one. And the younger one, his mouth open, was for a few moments unable to talk.

"It was not for me," he said at last. "I do not think so."

"Then I think that we should throw the letter into the bin, where it belongs," said Mma Makutsi. "Anonymous letters should always be ignored. The best place for them is the bin."

Nothing more was said. The apprentices returned to their work and Mma Makutsi sat at her desk and smiled. It was a wicked thing to have done, but she could not resist it. After all, one could not be good all the time, and occasional fun at the expense of another was harmless. She had told no lies, strictly speaking; she had seen a man walking away from the garage, but she had recognised him as one who did occasionally take a short-cut that way. The real sender of the letter was obviously some young girl who had been dared to write it by her friends. It was a piece of adolescent nonsense which everybody would soon forget about. And perhaps the boys had been taught some sort of lesson, about vanity certainly, but also, in an indirect way, about tolerance of the feelings of others, who might be a bit different from oneself. She doubted if they had learned the latter lesson, but it was there, she thought, visible if one bothered to think hard enough about it.

CHAPTER FOURTEEN

INSIDE THE HOUSE OF HOPE

MMA RAMOTSWE surveyed the House of Hope. It was a rather grand name for a modest bungalow which had been built in the early seventies, at a time when Gaborone was a small town, inching out from the cluster of buildings around Government Headquarters and the small square of shops nearby. These houses had been built for government employees or for expatriates who came to the country on short-term contracts. They were comfortable, and were large by the standards of most people's houses, but it seemed ambitious to use them for institutions, such as the House of Hope. But there was no choice, she imagined: larger buildings simply were not available, least of all to charities, which would have to scrimp and save to meet their costs.

There was a large garden, though, and this had been well-tended. In addition to a stand of healthy-looking paw-paw trees at the back, there were several clusters of bougainvillea and a mopipi tree. A vegetable garden, rather like the vegetable garden which Mr J.L.B. Matekoni had established in Mma Ramotswe's own yard, appeared to be growing beans and carrots with some success, although Mma Ramotswe reflected that in the case of carrots one could never really tell until one pulled them out of the ground. There were all sorts of insects which competed with us for carrots, and often what appeared from above to be a healthy plant would reveal itself as riddled with holes once pulled out of the soil.

There was a verandah to the side of the house, and somebody had thoughtfully placed shade netting over the side of this. That would be a good place to sit, thought Mma Ramotswe, and one might even drink tea there, on a hot afternoon, and feel the sun on one's face, but filtered by the shade netting. And then the thought occurred to her that all of Gaborone, the whole town, might be covered with shade netting, held aloft on great poles, and that this would keep the town cool and hold in the water which people put on their plants. It would be comfortable under this shade netting in summer, and then when winter came, and the air was cooler, they could roll back the shade netting to let in the winter sun, which would warm them, like the smile of an old friend. It was such a good idea, and it would surely not be too expensive for a country that had all those diamonds, but she knew that nobody would ever take it seriously. So they would continue to complain about the hot weather when it was hot and about the cold weather when it was cold.

The front door of the House of Hope opened immediately into the living room. This was a large room for that style of house, but the immediate and overwhelming impression it gave Mma Ramotswe was one of clutter. There were three or four chairs in the centre of the room—tightly arranged in a circle—and around them there were tables, storage boxes, and, here and there, a suit-case. On the wall, fixed with drawing pins, were pictures ripped from magazines; pictures of families and of mothers and chil-dren; of Mother Teresa with her characteristic headscarf; of Nel-son Mandela waving to a crowd; and of a line of African nuns, all clad in white, walking down a path through thick undergrowth, their hands joined in prayer. Mma Ramotswe's eye dwelt on the picture of the nuns. Where was the photograph taken, and where were these ladies going? They looked so peaceful, she thought, that perhaps it did not matter whether they were going anywhere, or nowhere in particular. People sometimes walked simply because walking was an enjoyable thing to do, and better than standing still, perhaps, if that was all you otherwise had to do. Sometimes she herself walked around her garden for no reason, and found it very relaxing, as perhaps it was for those nuns.

"You are interested in the pictures," said Mr Bobologo, behind her. "We think that it is important that these bar girls should be reminded of a better life. They can sit here and look at the pictures."

Mma Ramotswe nodded. She was not convinced that it would be much fun for a bar girl, or for anybody else for that matter, to be sitting on one of those chairs in that crowded room, looking at these pictures from the magazines. But then it would be better than listening to Mr Bobologo, she thought.

Mr Bobologo now came to Mma Ramotswe's side and pointed in the direction of the corridor that led off the living room. "I will be happy to show you the dormitories," he said. "We may find some of the bad girls in their rooms."

Mma Ramotswe raised an eyebrow. It was not very tactful of him to call them bad girls, even if they were. People rose to the descriptions of themselves, and it might have been better, she thought, to call them young ladies, in the hope that they might behave as young ladies behaved. But then, to be realistic, they probably would not behave that way, as it took a great deal to change somebody's ways.

The corridor was tidy enough, with only a small bookcase along one wall and the floor well-polished with that fresh-smelling polish that Mma Ramotswe's maid, Rose, so liked to use. They stopped outside a half-open bedroom door and Mr Bobologo knocked upon this before he pushed it open.

Mma Ramotswe looked inside. There were two bunk-beds in the room, both of them triple-deckers. The top bed was just below the ceiling, barely allowing enough space for anybody to fit in. Mma Ramotswe reflected that she herself would never fit in that space, but then these girls were younger, and some of them might be quite small.

There were three girls in the room, two lying fully clothed on the lower bunks and one wearing a dressing gown, and sitting on a middle bunk, her legs hanging down over the edge. As Mr Bobologo and Mma Ramotswe entered the room, they stared at them, not with any great interest, but with a rather vacant look.

"This lady is a visitor," Mr Bobologo announced, somewhat obviously, thought Mma Ramotswe.

One of the girls muttered something, which may have been a greeting but which was difficult to make out. The other one on the lower bunk nodded her head, while the girl sitting on the middle bunk managed a weak smile.

"You have a nice house here," said Mma Ramotswe. "Are you happy?"

The girls exchanged glances.

"Yes," said Mr Bobologo. "They are very happy."

Mma Ramotswe watched the girls, who did not appear inclined to contradict Mr Bobologo.

"And do you get good food here, ladies?" she asked.

"Very good food," said Mr Bobologo. "These good-time bar girls do not eat properly. They just drink dangerous liquor. When they are here they are given good, Botswana cooking. The food is very healthy."

"It is good to hear you telling me all this," Mma Ramotswe said, pointedly addressing her remark to the girls.

"That is all right," said Mr Bobologo. "We are happy to talk to visitors." He touched Mma Ramotswe's elbow and pointed out into the corridor. "I must show you the kitchen," he said. "And we must allow these girls to get on with their work."

It was not very apparent to Mma Ramotswe what this work was, and she had to suppress a smile as they walked back down the corridor towards the kitchen. He really was a most irritating man, this Mr Bobologo, with his tendency to speak for others and his one-track mind. Mma Holonga had struck Mma Ramotswe as being a reasonable woman, and yet she was seriously entertaining Mr Bobologo as a suitor, which seemed very strange. Surely Mma Holonga, with her wealth and position, could find somebody better than this curious teacher with his ponderous, didactic style.

They now stood at the door of the kitchen, in which two young women, barefoot and wearing light pink housecoats, were chopping vegetables on a large wooden chopping board. A pot of stew was boiling on the stove—boiling too vigorously, thought Mma Ramotswe—and a large cup of tea was cooling on the table. It would be good to be offered tea, she thought longingly, and that very cup looked just right.

"These girls are chopping vegetables," said Mr Bobologo solemnly. "And there is stew for our meal tonight."

"So I see," said Mma Ramotswe. "And I see, too, that they have just made tea."

"It is better for them to drink tea than strong liquor," intoned Mr Bobologo, looking disapprovingly at one of the girls, who cast her eyes downwards, in shame.

"Those are my views too," said Mma Ramotswe. "Tea refreshes. It clears the mind. Tea is good at any time of the day, but especially at mid-day, when it is so hot." She paused, and then added, "As it is today."

"You are right, Mma," said Mr Bobologo. "I am a great drinker of tea. I cannot understand why anybody would want to drink anything else when there is tea to be had. I have never been able to understand that."

Mma Ramotswe now used an expression which is common in Setswana and which indicates understanding, and firm endorsement of what another has said. "Eee, Rra," she said, with great depth of feeling, drawing out the vowels. If anything could convey to this man that she needed a cup of tea, this would. But it did not.

"This habit of drinking coffee is a very bad thing," went on Mr Bobologo. "Tea is better for the heart than coffee is. People who drink coffee strain their hearts. Tea has a calming effect on the heart. It makes the heart go more slowly. Thump, thump. That is what the heart should sound like. I have always said that."

"Yes," agreed Mma Ramotswe, weakly. "That is very true."

"That is why I am in favour of tea," pronounced Mr Bobologo with an air of finality, as might a speaker at a kgotla meeting make his concluding statement.

They stood there in silence. Mr Bobologo looked at the girls, who were still chopping vegetables with an air of studied concentration. Mma Ramotswe looked at the cup of tea. And the girls looked at the vegetables.

AFTER THEY had finished inspecting the kitchen—which was very clean, Mma Ramotswe noticed—they went out and sat on the verandah. There was still no tea, and when Mma Ramotswe, in a last desperate bid, mentioned that she was thirsty, a glass of water was called for. She sipped on this in a resigned way, imagining that it was bush tea, which helped slightly, but not a great deal.

"Now that you have seen the House of Hope," said Mr Bobologo, "you can ask me anything you like about it. Or you can tell me what you think. I don't mind. We have nothing to hide in the House of Hope."

Mma Ramotswe lifted her glass to her lips, noticing the greasy fingerprints around its rim, the fingerprints of those girls in the kitchen, she imagined. But this did not concern her. We all have fingerprints, after all.

"I think that this is a very good place," she began. "You are doing very good work."

"Yes, I am," said Mr Bobologo.

Mma Ramotswe looked out at the garden, at the rows of beans. A large black dung beetle was optimistically rolling a tiny trophy, a fragment of manure from the vegetable beds, back towards its home somewhere—a small bit of nature struggling with another small bit of nature, but as important as anything else in the world.

She turned to Mr Bobologo. "I was wondering, Rra," she began. "I was wondering why the girls come here. And why do they stay, if they want to be bar girls in the first place?"

Mr Bobologo nodded. This was clearly the obvious question to ask. "Some of them are very young and are sent here by the social work department or the police when they see them going into bars. Those girls have to stay, or the police will take them back to their village.

"Then there are the other bad girls, the ones our people meet down at the bus station or outside the bars. They may have nowhere to stay. They may be hungry. They may have been beaten up by some man. They are ready to come here then."

Mma Ramotswe listened carefully. The House of Hope

might be a rather dispiriting place, but it was better than the alternative.

"This is very interesting. Most of us are doing nothing about these things. You are doing something. That is very good." She paused. "But how did you come to do this work, Rra? Why do you give up all your time to this thing? You are a busy teacher, and you have much to do at the school. Instead, you very kindly come and give up all your time to this House of Hope."

Mr Bobologo thought for a moment. Mma Ramotswe noticed that his hands were clasped together; her question had unsettled him.

"I will tell you something, Mma," he said after a few moments. "I would not like you to speak about it, please. Will you give me your word that you will not speak about it?"

Instinctively Mma Ramotswe nodded, immediately realising that this would put her in difficulty if he said something that she needed to report to her client. But she had agreed to keep his secret, and she would honour that.

Mr Bobologo spoke quietly. "Something happened to me, Mma. Something happened some years ago, and I have not forgotten this thing. I had a daughter, you see, by my wife who is late. She was our first born, and our only child. I was very proud of her, as only a father can be proud. She was clever and did well at Gaborone Secondary School.

"Then one day she came back from school, and she was a different girl. Just like that. She paid no attention to me and she started to go out at night. I tried to keep her in and she would scream at me and stamp her feet. I did not know what to do. I could not raise a hand to her, as there was no mother, and a father does not strike a motherless child. I tried to reason with her, and she just said that I was an old man and I did not understand the things that she now understood.

"And then she left. She was just sixteen when this happened. She left, and I looked everywhere and asked everybody about her. Until one day I heard that she had been seen over the border, down in Mafikeng, and that this place where she had been seen, this place . . ." He faltered, and Mma Ramotswe reached out to him, in a gesture of sympathy and reassurance.

"You can carry on when you are ready, Rra," she said. But she already knew what he was going to say and he need not have continued.

"This place was a bar down there. I went there and my heart was hammering within me. I could not believe that my daughter would be in such a place. But she was, and she did not want to talk to me. I cried out to her and a man with a broken nose, a young man in a smart suit, a tsotsi type, came and threatened me. He said, *Go home, uncle. Your daughter is not your property. Go home, or pay for one of these girls, like everybody else.* Those were his words, Mma."

Mma Ramotswe was silent. Her hand was on his shoulder, and it remained there.

Mr Bobologo raised his head and looked up into the sky, high above the shade netting. "And so I said to myself that I would work to help these girls, because there are other fathers, just like me, who have this awful thing happen to them. These men are my brothers, Mma. I hope that you understand that."

Mma Ramotswe swallowed. "I understand very well," she said. "I understand. Your heart is broken, Rra. I understand that."

"It is broken inside me," echoed Mr Bobologo. "You are right about that, Mma."

There was not much else to be said, and they made their way down the path to Mma Ramotswe's tiny white van, parked under a tree. But as they walked, Mma Ramotswe decided to ask another question, more by way of making conversation than to elicit information.

"What are your plans for the House of Hope, Rra?"

Mr Bobologo turned and looked back at the house. "We are going to build an extension there at the side," he said. "We shall have new showers and a room where the girls can learn sewing. That is what we are going to do."

"That will be expensive," said Mma Ramotswe. "Extensions always seem to cost more than the house itself. These builders are greedy men."

Mr Bobologo laughed. "But I will shortly be in a position to pay," he said. "I think that I may be a rich man before too long."

Had Mma Ramotswe been less experienced than she was, had she not been the founder of the No. 1 Ladies' Detective Agency, this remark would have caused her to falter, to miss her step. But she was an experienced woman, whose job had shown her all of human life, and so she appeared quite unperturbed by what he had said. But these last few words that Mr Bobologo uttered—every one of them—fell into the pond of memory with a resounding splash.

CHAPTER FIFTEEN

BAD MEN ARE JUST
LITTLE BOYS, UNDERNEATH

THE FOLLOWING morning at Tlokweng Road Speedy Motors, when the morning rush had abated, Mma Ramotswe decided to stretch her legs. She had been sitting at her desk, dictating a letter to a client, while Mma Makutsi's pencil moved over the page of her notepad with a satisfactory squeak. Shorthand had been one of her strongest subjects at the Botswana Secretarial College, and she enjoyed taking dictation.

"Many secretaries these days don't have shorthand," Mma Makutsi had remarked to Mma Ramotswe. "Can you believe it, Mma? They call themselves secretaries, and they don't have shorthand. What would Mr Pitman think?"

"Who is this Mr Pitman?" asked Mma Ramotswe. "What is he thinking about?"

"He is a very famous man," said Mma Makutsi. "He invented shorthand. He wrote books about it. He is one of the great heroes of the secretarial movement."

"I see," said Mma Ramotswe. "Perhaps they should put up a statue to him at the Botswana Secretarial College. In that way he would be remembered."

"That is a very good idea," said Mma Makutsi. "But I do not

think they will do it. They would have to raise the money from the graduates, and I do not think that some of those girls—the ones who do not know anything about shorthand, and who only managed to get something like fifty per cent in the exams—I do not think they would pay."

Mma Ramotswe nodded vaguely. She was not particularly interested in the affairs of the Botswana Secretarial College, although she always listened politely when Mma Makutsi sounded off about such matters. Most people had something in their lives that was particularly important to them, and she supposed that the Botswana Secretarial College was as good a cause as any. What was it in her own case, she wondered? Tea? Surely she had something more important than that; but what? She looked at Mma Makutsi, as if for inspiration, but none came, and she decided to return to the subject later, in an idle moment, when one had time for this sort of unsettling philosophical speculation.

Now, the morning's dictation finished and the letters duly signed, Mma Ramotswe arose from her desk, leaving Mma Makutsi to address the envelopes and find the right postage stamps in the mail drawer. Mma Ramotswe glanced out of the window; it was precisely the sort of morning she appreciated—not too hot, and yet with an empty, open sky, flooded with sunlight. This was the sort of morning that birds liked, she thought; when they could stretch their wings and sing out; the sort of morning when you could fill your lungs with air and inhale nothing but the fragrance of acacia and the grass and the sweet, sweet smell of cattle.

She left the office by the back door and stood outside, her eyes closed, the sun on her face. It would be good to be back in Mochudi, she thought, to be sitting in front of somebody's house peeling vegetables, or crocheting something perhaps. That's what she had done when she was a girl, and had sat with her cousin, who was adept at crocheting and made place mat after place mat in fine white thread; so many place mats that every table in Botswana could have been covered twice over, but which somebody, somewhere, bought and sold on. These days she had no time for crocheting, and she wondered whether she would even remember how to do it. Of course, crocheting was like riding a bicycle, which people said that you never forgot how to do once you had learned it. But was that true? Surely there were things that one might forget how to do, if enough time elapsed between the occasions on which one had to do whatever it was that one had forgotten. Mma Ramotswe had once come across somebody who had forgotten his Setswana, and she had been astonished, and shocked. This person had gone to live in Mozambique as a young man and had spoken Tsonga there, and had learned Portuguese too. When he came back to Botswana, thirty years later, it seemed as if he were a foreigner, and she had seen him look puzzled when people used quite simple, everyday Setswana words. To lose your own language was like forgetting your mother, and as sad, in a way. We must not lose Setswana, she thought, even if we speak a great deal of English these days, because that would be like losing part of one's soul.

Mma Makutsi, of course, had another language tucked away in her background. Her mother had been a speaker of Ikalanga, because she had come from Marapong, where they spoke a dialect of Ikalanga called Lilima. That made life very complicated, thought Mma Ramotswe, because that meant that she spoke a minor version of a minor language. Mma Makutsi had been brought up speaking both Setswana, her father's language, and this strange version of Ikalanga, and then had learned English at school, because that was how one got on in life. You could never even get to the Botswana Secretarial College if you spoke no English, and you would certainly never get anywhere near ninety-seven per cent unless your English was almost faultless, like the English that schoolteachers *used* to speak.

Mma Ramotswe had more or less forgotten that Mma Makutsi spoke Ikalanga until one day she had used an Ikalanga word in the middle of a sentence, and it had stuck out.

"I have hurt my gumbo," Mma Makutsi had said.

Mma Ramotswe had looked at her in surprise. "Your gumbo?"

"Yes," said Mma Makutsi. "When I was walking to work today, I stepped into a pothole and hurt my gumbo." She paused, noticing the look of puzzlement on Mma Ramotswe's face. Then she realised. "I'm sorry," she said. "*Gumbo* is foot in Ikalanga. If you speak Ikalanga, your foot is your gumbo."

"I see," said Mma Ramotswe. "That is a very strange word. Gumbo."

"It is not strange," said Mma Makutsi, slightly defensively. "There are many different words for foot. It is *foot* in English. In Setswana it is *lonao,* and in Ikalanga it is *gumbo,* which is what it really is."

Mma Ramotswe laughed. "There is no *real* word for foot. You cannot say it is really gumbo, because that is true only for Ikalanga-speaking feet. Each foot has its own name, depending on the language which the foot's mother spoke. That is the way it works, Mma Makutsi."

That had ended the conversation, and no more was said of gumbos.

These, and other, thoughts went through Mma Ramotswe's head as she stood outside the office that morning, stretching, and allowing her mind to wander this way and that. After a few minutes, though, she decided that it was time to get back into the office. Mma Makutsi would have finished addressing the letters by now, and she wanted to tell her about yesterday's visit to the House of Hope. There was a lot to be said about that, and she thought it would be useful to discuss it with her assistant. Mma Makutsi often came up with very shrewd observations, although in the case of Mr Bobologo no particular shrewdness was required to work out what his motives were. And yet, and yet . . . One could not say that he was an insincere man. He was patently sincere when it came to bar girls, but marriage, perhaps, was another matter. Mma Makutsi might have valuable insights into this, and this would help clarify the situation in Mma Ramotswe's mind.

Mma Ramotswe opened her eyes and started to make her way back into the office. She was intercepted in the doorway, though, by Mma Makutsi, who looked anxious.

"There is something wrong," Mma Makutsi whispered to her. "There is something wrong with Mr J.L.B. Matekoni. Back there." She gestured towards the garage. "There is something wrong with him."

"Has he hurt himself?" Mma Ramotswe always dreaded the possibility of an accident, particularly with those careless apprentices being allowed to raise cars on ramps and do other dangerous things. Mechanics hurt themselves, it was well-known, just as butchers often had parts of fingers missing, a sight which always made Mma Ramotswe's blood run cold, although the enthusiasm of the butchers for their great chopping knives—the guilty blades, no doubt—seemed undiminished.

Mma Makutsi set her mind at rest. "No, there has not been an accident. But I saw him sitting in the garage with his head in his hands. He looked very miserable, and he hardly greeted me when I walked past him. I think something has happened."

This was not good news. Even if there had been no accident, Mr J.L.B. Matekoni's recovery from his depressive illness was recent enough to make any apparent drop in mood a cause for concern. Dr Moffat, who had treated Mr J.L.B. Matekoni during his illness—with the assistance of Mma Potokwane, it must be recalled, who had taken Mr J.L.B. Matekoni in hand and made him take his pills—had warned that these illnesses could recur. Mma Ramotswe remembered his very words: "You must be watchful, Mma Ramotswe," the doctor had said, in that kind voice he used when he spoke to everybody, even to his rather ill-tempered brown spaniel. "You must be watchful because this illness is like a dark cloud in the sky. It is often there, just over the horizon, but it can blow up very quickly. Watch, and tell me if anything happens."

So far, the recovery had seemed complete, and Mr J.L.B. Matekoni had been as equable and as constant as he always had been. There had been no sign of the lassitude that had come with the illness; no sign of the dark, introspective brooding which had so reduced him. But perhaps this was it coming back. Perhaps the cloud had blown over and had covered his sky.

Mma Ramotswe thanked Mma Makutsi and made her way into the garage. The two apprentices were bent over the engine of a car, spanners in hand, and Mr J.L.B. Matekoni was sitting on his old canvas chair near the compressor, his head sunk in his hands, just as Mma Makutsi had seen him.

"Now then, Mr J.L.B. Matekoni," said Mma Ramotswe breezily. "You seem to be thinking very hard about something. Can I make you a cup of tea to help you think?"

Mr J.L.B. Matekoni looked up, and as he did so Mma Ramotswe realised, with relief, that the illness had not returned. He looked worried, certainly, but it was a very different look from the haunted look he had developed during the illness. This was a real worry, she thought; not a worry about shadows and imaginary wrongs and dying; all those things which had so tormented him when he was ill.

"Yes, I am thinking," he said. "I am thinking that I have dug myself into a mess. I am like a potato in . . ." He stopped, unable to complete the metaphor.

"Like a potato?" asked Mma Ramotswe.

"Like a potato in a . . ." He stopped again. "I don't know. But I have done a very foolish thing in involving myself in this business."

Mma Ramotswe was perplexed, and asked him what business he meant.

"This whole business with that butcher's car," he said. "I went round to First Class Motors yesterday afternoon."

"Ah!" said Mma Ramotswe, and thought: this is my fault. I urged him to go and now this has happened. So, rather than say Ah! again, she said, "Oh!"

"Yes," went on Mr J.L.B. Matekoni miserably. "I went up there yesterday afternoon. The man who runs the place was at a funeral in Molepolole, and so I spoke to one of his assistants. And this man said that he had seen the butcher's car round at my garage and he had mentioned it to his boss, who was very cross. He said that I was taking his clients, and that he was going to come round and see me about it this morning, when he arrived back from Molepolole. He said that his boss was going to 'sort me out.' That's what he said, Mma Ramotswe. Those were his words. I didn't even have the chance to complain, as I had intended to. I didn't even have the chance."

Mma Ramotswe folded her arms. "Who is this man?" she snapped angrily. "What is his name, and who does he think he is? Where is he from?"

Mr J.L.B. Matekoni sighed. "He is called Molefi. He is a horrible man from Tlokweng. People are scared of him. He gives mechanics a bad name."

Mma Ramotswe said nothing for a moment. She felt sorry for

Mr J.L.B. Matekoni, who was a very peaceful man and who did not like conflict. He was not one to start an argument, and yet she rather wished that he would stand up to this Molefi man a bit more. Such people were bullies and the only thing to do was to stand up to them. If only Mr J.L.B. Matekoni were a bit braver . . . Did she really want him to fight, though? It was quite out of character, and that was just as well. She could not abide men who threw their weight around, and that was one of the reasons why she so admired Mr J.L.B. Matekoni. Although he was physically strong from all that lifting of engines, he was gentle. And she loved him for that, as did so many others.

She unfolded her arms and walked over to stand beside Mr J.L.B. Matekoni. "When is this man coming?" she asked.

"Any time now. They said this morning. That is all they said."

"I see." She turned away, intending to go over to the apprentices and have a word with them. They would have to rally round to deal with this Molefi person. They were young men . . . She stopped. Tlokweng. Mr J.L.B. Matekoni had said that Molefi was from Tlokweng, and Tlokweng was where the orphan farm was, and the orphan farm made her think of Mma Potokwane.

She turned back again, ignoring the apprentices, and walked briskly back into her office. Mma Makutsi looked up at her expectantly as she came in.

"Is he all right? I was worried."

"He is fine," she said. "He is worried about something. That man at First Class Motors has been threatening him. That's what's going on."

Mma Makutsi whistled softly, as she sometimes did in moments of crisis. "That is very bad, Mma. That is very bad."

Mma Ramotswe nodded. "Mma Makutsi," she said. "I am going out to Tlokweng right now. This very minute. Please telephone Mma Potokwane and tell her that I am coming to fetch her in my van and that we need her help. Please do that right now. I am going."

WHEN MMA RAMOTSWE arrived at the orphan farm, Mma Potokwane was not in her office. The door was open, but the large, rather shabby chair in which Mma Potokwane was often to be found—when she was not bustling round the kitchens or the houses—was empty. Mma Ramotswe rushed outside again and looked about anxiously. It had not occurred to her that Mma Potokwane might not be found; she was always on duty, it seemed. And yet she could be in town, doing some shopping, or she could even be far away, down in Lobatse, perhaps, picking up some new orphan.

"Mma Ramotswe?"

She gave a start, looking about her. It was Mma Potokwane's voice, but where was she?

"Here!" came the voice. "Under this tree! Here I am, Mma Ramotswe."

The matron of the orphan farm was in the shade of a large mango tree, merging with the shadows. Mma Ramotswe had looked right past her, but now Mma Potokwane stepped out from under the drooping branches of the tree.

"I have been watching a special mango," she said. "It is almost ready and I have told the children that they are not to pick it. I am keeping it for my husband, who likes to eat a good mango." She dusted her hands on her skirts as she walked towards Mma Ramotswe. "Would you like to see this mango, Mma Ramotswe?" she asked. "It is very fine. Very yellow now."

"You are very kind, Mma," called out Mma Ramotswe. "I will

come and see it some other time, I think. Right now there is something urgent to talk to you about. Something very urgent."

Mma Potokwane joined her friend outside the office, and Mma Ramotswe quickly explained that she needed her to come to the garage, "to help with Mr J.L.B. Matekoni." Mma Potokwane listened gravely and nodded her agreement. They could go straight away, she said. No, she would not need to fetch anything from her office. "All I need is my voice," she said, pointing to her chest. "And it is all there. Ready to be used."

They travelled back to the garage in the tiny white van, now heavily laden and riding low on its shock absorbers. Mma Ramotswe drove more quickly than she normally did, sounding the horn impatiently at indolent donkeys and children on wobbling cycles. There was only one hold-up—a small herd of rickety cattle, badly looked after by all appearances, which blocked the road until Mma Potokwane opened her window and shouted at them in a stentorian voice. The cattle looked surprised, and indignant, but they moved, and the tiny white van continued its journey.

They drew up at Tlokweng Road Speedy Motors a few minutes after the arrival of Molefi. A large red truck was parked outside the garage, blocking the entrance, and on this was written FIRST CLASS MOTORS in ostentatious lettering. Mma Potokwane, to whom the situation had been explained by Mma Ramotswe on the way back, saw this and snorted.

"Big letters," she murmured. "Big nothing."

Mma Ramotswe smiled. She was sure that the summoning of Mma Potokwane was the right thing to do and this remark made her even more certain. Now, as they negotiated their way round the aggressively parked truck and she saw Molefi standing in front of Mr J.L.B. Matekoni, who was looking down at the ground as his visitor remonstrated with him, she realised that they had not arrived a minute too early.

Mma Potokwane bustled forward. "So," she said. "Who do we find here in Mr J.L.B. Matekoni's garage? Molefi? It's you, isn't it? You've come to discuss some difficult mechanical problem with Mr J.L.B. Matekoni, have you? Come for his advice?"

Molefi looked round and glowered. "I am here on business, Mma. It's business between me and Mr J.L.B. Matekoni." His tone was rude and he compounded the offence by turning his back on Mma Potokwane and facing Mr J.L.B. Matekoni again. Mma Potokwane glanced at Mma Ramotswe, who shook her head in disapproval of Molefi's rudeness.

"Excuse me, Rra," said Mma Potokwane, stepping forward. "I think that perhaps you might have forgotten who I am, but I certainly know exactly who you are."

Molefi turned around in irritation. "Listen, Mma . . ."

"No, you listen to me, Rra," Mma Potokwane said, her voice rising sharply. "I know you, Herbert Molefi. I know your mother. She is my friend. And I have often felt sorry for her, with a son like you."

Molefi opened his mouth to speak, but no sound came.

"Oh yes," went on Mma Potokwane, shaking a finger at him. "You were a bad little boy, and now you are a bad man. You are just a bully, that's what you are. And I have heard this thing about the butcher's car. Oh, yes, I have heard it. And I wonder whether your mother knows it, or your uncles? Do they know it?"

Molefi's collapse was sudden and complete. Mma Ramotswe watched the effect of these words and saw the burly figure shrink visibly in the face of Mma Potokwane's tongue-lashing.

"No? They have not heard about it?" she pressed on. "Well, I think I might just let them know. And you, you, Herbert Molefi, who thinks that he can go round bullying people like Mr J.L.B.

Matekoni here, had better think again. Your mother can still tell you a thing or two, can't she? And your uncles. They will not be pleased and they might just give their cattle to somebody else when they die, might they not? I think so, Rra. I think so."

"Now, Mma," said Molefi. "I am just talking to Mr J.L.B. Matekoni, that is all I am doing."

"Pah!" retorted Mma Potokwane. "Don't you try to tell me your lies. You just shut that useless mouth of yours for a little while and let Mr J.L.B. Matekoni tell you what to do about that poor man you've cheated. And I'll just stand here and listen, just in case. Then we'll think about whether your people out at Tlokweng need to be told about this."

Molefi was silent, and he remained silent while Mr J.L.B. Matekoni quietly and reasonably told him that he would have to make a refund to the butcher and that he should be careful in the future, as other garages in the town would be watching what he did. "You let us all down, you see," said Mr J.L.B. Matekoni. "If one mechanic cheats, then all mechanics are blamed. That is what happens, and that is why you should change your ways."

"Yes," said Mma Ramotswe, making her first contribution. "You just be careful in future, or Mma Potokwane will hear of it. Do you understand?"

Molefi nodded silently.

"Has a goat eaten your tongue?" asked Mma Ramotswe.

"No," said Molefi quietly. "I understand what you have said, Mma."

"Good," said Mma Potokwane. "Now the best thing you can do is to move that truck of yours and get back to your garage. I think that you will have an envelope in your office. That will do for the letter you are going to write to that man in Lobatse." She paused before adding, "And send me a copy, if you don't mind."

There was not much more to be said after that. Molefi reversed his truck and drove angrily away. Mr J.L.B. Matekoni thanked Mma Potokwane, rather sheepishly, thought Mma Ramotswe, and the two women went into the office of the No. 1 Ladies' Detective Agency, where Mma Makutsi had boiled the kettle for tea. Mma Makutsi had listened to the encounter from the doorway. She was somewhat in awe of Mma Potokwane, but now she asked her a question.

"Is his mother that fierce?"

"I have no idea," said Mma Potokwane. "I've only seen his mother; I've never met her, and I took a bit of a risk with that. But usually bullies have severe mothers and bad fathers, and they are usually frightened of them. That is why they are bullies, I think. There is something wrong at home. I have found that with children in general and this applies to men as well. I think that I shall have to write about that if I ever write a book about how to run an orphan farm."

"You must write that book, Mma," urged Mma Ramotswe. "I would read it, even if I was not planning to run an orphan farm."

"Thank you," said Mma Potokwane. "Maybe I shall do that one day. But at the moment I am so busy looking after all those orphans and making tea and baking fruit cake and all those things. There seems very little time for writing books."

"That is a pity," said Mma Makutsi. It had just occurred to her that she might write a book herself, if Mma Potokwane, of all people, was considering doing so. *The Principles of Typing*, perhaps, although that was not perhaps the most exciting title one might imagine. *How to Get Ninety-Seven Per Cent*. Now that was much, much better, and would be bought by all those people, those many, many people who would love to get ninety-seven per cent in whatever it was that they were doing and who knew that perhaps they never would. At least they could hope, which was an important thing. We must be able to hope. We simply must.

CHAPTER SIXTEEN

MMA POTOKWANE AND MMA
RAMOTSWE DISCUSS MARRIAGE

THESE MATTERS were distractions, of course, but at least the matter of the butcher's car was now sorted out and Mr J.L.B. Matekoni, only so recently worried on two fronts—the parachute jump and First Class Motors—could now look forward to the immediate future with greater equanimity. Mma Potokwane had been magnificent, as she always was, and had dispatched the bullying Herbert Molefi with the same ease as she dealt with ten-year-old bullies. She had been happy to do this, as she owed Mr J.L.B. Matekoni a great deal, with his constant and unquestioning availability to fix bits and pieces of machinery on the orphan farm. And Mma Potokwane, like everybody else who came into contact with him, recognised in Mr J.L.B. Matekoni those qualities which endeared him to so many and which meant that most people would do anything for him: his courtesy, his reliability, his sheer decency. If only all men, or even more men, were like that, thought Mma Potokwane, indeed thought all the women of Botswana. If only you could trust men in the same way in which you could trust a close woman friend; instead of which, men tended to let women down, not always deliberately, but just because they were selfish or they became bored, or their heads were turned in some way. It was very easy to turn a man's head; a glamorous woman could do it just by looking at a man and lowering her eyelids once or twice. That could make an apparently steadfast man quite unpredictable, particularly if that man were of an age where he was starting to feel unsure of himself as a man.

Mma Ramotswe was lucky to be engaged to Mr J.L.B. Matekoni, thought Mma Potokwane. He was exactly the right choice for her, as she was a fine woman and she deserved a good man like Mr J.L.B. Matekoni with whom to share her life. It was hard being a woman by oneself, particularly when one was in a job such as Mma Ramotswe's, and it was important to have a man on whom one could call for assistance and support. So Mma Ramotswe had made a wise choice, even if all those years ago she had shown a distinct lack of judgment in marrying Note Mokoti, the trumpet player. Mokoti, Matekoni: similar names, reflected Mma Potokwane, but how different the men who bore the names.

Of course there was the question of the length of the engagement and the slowness with which preparations were being made for the wedding, indeed if any preparations were being made at all. This was a puzzle to Mma Potokwane, and while Mma Makutsi made tea that day, after the disposal of Herbert Molefi, Mma Potokwane decided to raise the matter with Mma Ramotswe. She was direct rather than allusive; rather too direct, thought Mma Makutsi, who listened but did not say anything. She tended to feel inhibited in the presence of Mma Potokwane, largely because she felt the other woman was so much more confident and experienced than she was. There was also an element of disapproval in Mma Makutsi's attitude—not that she would ever have expressed it. She thought that Mma Potokwane was too ready to take advantage of Mr J.L.B. Matekoni's good nature. The kindness of men like that could be exploited by forceful women, and there was no doubt but that Mma Potokwane was in the vanguard of the forceful women of Botswana, their very standard bearer, their champion.

So Mma Makutsi said nothing, but listened very carefully as Mma Potokwane raised the subject of marriage and weddings, virtually under the nose of Mr J.L.B. Matekoni, who had resumed work on a car next door. And what if he had walked in the door and heard her speaking in these terms; what then? Mma Makutsi was astonished at the matron's tactlessness.

"Such a very good man," came the opening gambit. "He has been very helpful to us at the orphan farm. All the children love him and call him their special uncle. So there he is an uncle, but not yet a husband!"

Mma Ramotswe smiled. "Yes, he is a fine man. And he will make a good husband one day. That is why I agreed to his proposal."

Mma Potokwane looked at her fingernails, as if absorbed by some cuticular matter. "One day?" she said. "Which day? When is this day you are talking about? Next week, do you think? Or next year?"

"Not next week," said Mma Ramotswe evenly. "Maybe next year. Who knows?"

Mma Potokwane was quick to press home on this question. "But does he know? That's the important thing. Does Mr J.L.B. Matekoni know?"

Mma Ramotswe made a gesture which indicated that she did not know the answer and that indeed the matter was not important as far as she was concerned. "Mr J.L.B. Matekoni is not a man who makes hasty decisions. He likes to think about things for a long time."

Mma Potokwane shook her head. "That is a weakness, Mma Ramotswe," she said. "I'm sorry to have to say this, but there are some men who need to be organised by women. Every woman

knows this. It is only now, in these modern days, with men getting ideas about running their lives without any help from
women—those dangerous, bad ideas—it is only now that we see
how much these poor men need our assistance. It is a very sad
thing."

"I don't know about that," countered Mma Ramotswe. "I
know that ladies have to help men in many things. Sometimes it
is necessary to push men a little bit. But one should not take it
too far."

"Well it's not going too far to push men to the altar," retorted
Mma Potokwane. "Women have always done that, and that is how
marriages take place. If you left it up to men, they would never
get there. Nobody would be married. You have to remind men to
get married."

Mma Ramotswe looked at her guest thoughtfully. Should she
allow Mma Potokwane to help her to get Mr J.L.B. Matekoni a little bit further along the road to matrimony? It was awkward for
her; she did not want him to form the impression that she was
interfering too much in his life; men did not like that, and many
men would simply leave if they felt this was happening. At the
same time, if Mr J.L.B. Matekoni did need slight prompting, it
would be easier for this to come from Mma Potokwane, who had a
long history of pushing Mr J.L.B. Matekoni about, most of it with
considerable success. One only had to remember the matter of
that old pump at the orphan farm which she had cajoled him into
maintaining well beyond the point where he had formed the professional opinion that it should be scrapped. And one only had to
recall the recent instance of the parachute jump, which was
another example of Mr J.L.B. Matekoni being made to agree to
something to which he did not wish to agree. Perhaps there was a
case for assistance in this matter too . . .

No, no, no! thought Mma Makutsi, willing her employer not

to yield to the imprecations of the manipulative Mma Potokwane. She could see that Mma Ramotswe was tempted, and if only Mma Potokwane had not been there she would have urged Mma Ramotswe in the most vocal terms not to do anything which could have serious consequences for the engagement or, even more importantly, for Mr J.L.B. Matekoni's state of health. Dr Moffat had told them all that Mr J.L.B. Matekoni was not to be put under any stress, and what could be more stressful than to be the object of a determined campaign by Mma Potokwane? Look at that Herbert Molefi man, crushed by her tongue and unable to do anything to defend himself. If only the Botswana Defence Force could have seen it, thought Mma Makutsi, they would have signed her up immediately and made her a sergeant-major or a general or whatever they called those soldiers who ordered all the other soldiers about. Or even better, Mma Potokwane could have been used as a weapon to intimidate the enemy, whoever they were. They would see Mma Potokwane coming towards them and they would be incapable of doing anything, reduced by the sight to mute and helpless boys.

None of these thoughts reached Mma Ramotswe, although she did briefly glance across the room to where Mma Makutsi was busying herself with the tea. But Mma Makutsi was turned away at the time and Mma Ramotswe did not see her expression, so she had no idea of the other woman's feelings.

"Well," began Mma Ramotswe cautiously, "how would we help Mr J.L.B. Matekoni to make a decision? How would we do it?"

"We don't have to help him make any decision," replied Mma Potokwane firmly. "He has already made the decision to marry you, has he not? What is an engagement? It is an agreement to marry. That decision is made, Mma. No, all we have to do is to arrange for him to carry it out. We need to get a date, and then we need to make sure that he gets to the right place on the date. And in my view that means that we should make all the plans and then pick him up on the day and take him there. That's right, we'll *take* him there."

At this, Mma Makutsi spun round and stared at Mma Ramotswe open-mouthed. Surely Mma Ramotswe would see the danger in this? If you took a man to the church, he would simply run away. No man would be forced in this way, and certainly not a mature and intelligent man like Mr J.L.B. Matekoni. This was the stuff of disaster, and Mma Ramotswe should put a stop to these ridiculous fantasies at once. But instead—and here Mma Makutsi drew in her breath in astonishment—instead she was nodding her head in agreement!

"Good," said Mma Potokwane enthusiastically. "I can see that you agree with me. So now all we have to do is to plan the wedding and get everything ready—in secret of course—and then on the day get him into a suit somehow . . ."

"And how would you do that?" interrupted Mma Ramotswe. "You know the sort of clothes that Mr J.L.B. Matekoni normally wears. Those overalls. That old hat with grease round the rim. Those suede veldschoens. How will we get him out of those and into suitable clothes for church?"

"Leave that side of it to me," said Mma Potokwane confidently. "In fact, simply leave the whole thing to me. We can have the wedding out at the orphan farm. I will get my housemothers to cook all the food. I will make all the arrangements and all you will have to do is to get there at the time I will tell you. Then you will be married. I promise you."

Mma Ramotswe looked doubtful and was about to open her mouth to say something when Mma Potokwane continued. "You needn't worry, Mma Ramotswe. I am a very tactful person. I know how to do these things. You know that."

Mma Makutsi's eyes widened, but she knew that there was

no stopping Mma Potokwane now, and that events would run their course whatever she tried to do. And what was there for her to do? She could attempt to persuade Mma Ramotswe to forbid Mma Potokwane from proceeding with her plan, but that would be unlikely to happen once Mma Ramotswe had agreed to it. She could warn Mr J.L.B. Matekoni that he was in danger of being pushed into his own wedding, but then that would seem appallingly disloyal to Mma Ramotswe, and if she did that she might be responsible for his doing something really foolish, such as calling off the engagement altogether. No, there was only one thing for Mma Makutsi to do, and that was to keep out of the whole affair, although she would allow herself one remark, perhaps, just as an aside, to register her disapproval of the whole scheme.

Mma Potokwane did not stay long, but every minute of the visit seemed to drag terribly. An icy atmosphere had developed, with Mma Makutsi sitting in almost complete silence, responding to Mma Potokwane's remarks only in the briefest and most unhelpful of terms.

"You must be very busy," the matron said to her, pointing to the papers on her desk. "I have heard that you are a very efficient secretary. Perhaps you will come out to the orphan farm one day and sort out my office! That would be a good thing to do. You could have a big bonfire of all the spare papers. The children would like that."

"I am too busy," said Mma Makutsi. "Perhaps you should employ a secretary. There is a very fine secretarial college, you know, the Botswana Secretarial College. They will provide you with a name. They will also tell you what the right salary will be."

Mma Potokwane took a sip of her tea and looked at Mma Makutsi over the rim of the cup.

"Thank you, Mma," she said. "That is a good suggestion. But

of course we are an orphan farm and we do not have very much money for secretaries and the like. That is why kind people—people like Mr J.L.B. Matekoni—offer their services free."

"He is a kind man," agreed Mma Makutsi. "That is why people take advantage of him."

Mma Potokwane put down her cup and turned to Mma Ramotswe. "You are very lucky to have an assistant who can give you good advice," she said politely. "That must make your life easier."

Mma Ramotswe, who had been quite aware of the developing tension, did her best to smooth over the situation.

"Most tasks in this life are better done by two people," she said. "I am sure that you get a lot of support from the housemothers. I am sure that they have good advice to give too."

Mma Potokwane rose to her feet to leave. "Yes, Mma," she said, glancing at Mma Makutsi. "We must all help one another. That is very true."

One of the apprentices was detailed to drive Mma Potokwane back to the orphan farm, leaving Mma Ramotswe and Mma Makutsi alone in the office once again. Mma Makutsi, sitting at her desk, looked down at her shoes, as she often did in moments of crisis; her shoes, always her allies, but now so unhelpfully mute, as if to convey: *don't look at us, we said nothing. You were the one, Boss.* (In her mind, her shoes always addressed her as Boss, as the apprentices addressed Mr J.L.B. Matekoni. This was right for shoes, which should know their place.)

"I'm sorry, Mma," Mma Makutsi suddenly burst out. "I had to stand there making tea while that woman gave you that terrible, terrible advice. And I couldn't say anything because I always feel too small to say anything when she's around. She makes me feel as if I'm still six years old."

Mma Ramotswe looked at her assistant with concern. "She is

just trying to help. She's bossy, of course, but that is because she is a matron. Every matron is bossy; if they weren't then nothing would get done. Mma Potokwane's job is to be bossy. But she is just trying to help."

"But it won't help," wailed Mma Makutsi. "It won't help at all. You can't force Mr J.L.B. Matekoni to get married."

"Nobody's forcing him," said Mma Ramotswe. "He asked me to marry him. I said yes. He has never once, not once, said that he does not want to get married. Have you ever heard him say that? No, well there you are."

"But he will agree to a wedding one day," said Mma Makutsi. "You can wait."

"Can I, Mma?" said Mma Ramotswe quickly. "Can I wait forever? And why should I wait all this time and put up with all this uncertainty? My life is going past. Tick, tick. Like a clock that is running too fast. And all the time I remain an engaged lady. People are talking, believe me. They say: there's that lady who's engaged forever to Mr J.L.B. Matekoni. That's what they are saying."

Mma Makutsi was silent, and Mma Ramotswe continued, "I don't want to force Mr J.L.B. Matekoni to do anything he doesn't want to do. But in this case I think that there is some sort of block—there is some sort of reason why he cannot make up his mind. I think it is in his nature. Dr Moffat said that when people had that illness—that depression thing—then they might not be able to make decisions. Even when they seem quite well. Maybe there is a little corner of that in Mr J.L.B. Matekoni. So all we are trying to do is help him."

Mma Makutsi shook her head. "I don't know, Mma. You may be right, but I am very worried. I do not think that you should let Mma Potokwane stick her nose into this business."

"I understand what you are saying to me," said Mma Ramotswe. "But I have reached the end of waiting. I have waited,

waited, waited. No date has been mentioned. Nothing has been said. No cattle have been bought for the feast. No chairs have been fixed up. No aunties have been written to. Nothing has been done. Nothing. No lady can accept that, Mma."

Mma Makutsi again looked down at her shoes. This time the shoes were vocal: *you just be quiet now*, they said rather rudely.

CHAPTER SEVENTEEN

MR SPOKES SPOKESI, THE AIRWAVE RIDER

F MMA Ramotswe was still on the shelf, then the following day she was on the wall. She was sitting on the wall in question, the waist-high wall that surrounded the car park of Radio Gabs, enjoying the effervescent company of two seventeen-year-old girls. They were attractive girls, dressed in jeans and bright-coloured blouses that must have cost them a great deal, thought Mma Ramotswe; too much, in fact, because the most expensive parts of their outfit, the labels, were prominently displayed. Mma Ramotswe had never been able to understand why people wanted to have their labels on the outside. In her day, labels had been tucked in, which is where they belonged in her view. One did not walk around the town with one's birth certificate stuck on one's back; why then should clothes have their labels on the outside? It was a very vulgar display, she felt, but it did not really matter with these nice girls, who were talking so quickly and in such an amusing way about all the things which interested them, which was not very much, at the end of the day; in fact which was only one subject when one came to think of it, or two, possibly, if one included fashion.

"Some people say that there are no good-looking men in

Gaborone," said Constance, the girl sitting to Mma Ramotswe's right. "But I think that is nonsense. There are many good-looking men in Gaborone. I have seen hundreds, just in one day. Hundreds."

Her friend, Kokotso, looked dubious. "Oh?" she said. "Where can I go to see all these good-looking men? Is there a club for good-looking men maybe? Can I go and stand outside the door and watch?"

"There is no such club," laughed Constance. "And if there were, then the men would not be able to get near it, for all the girls standing at the door. It would not work."

Mma Ramotswe decided to join in. It was many years since she had participated in such a conversation, and she was beginning to enjoy it. "It all depends on what you mean by good-looking," she said. "Some men are good-looking in one department and not so good-looking in another. Some men have nice wide shoulders, but very thin legs. Very thin legs are not so good. I know one girl who left a good boyfriend because his legs were too thin."

"Ow!" exclaimed Kokotso. "That girl made a very bad move. If he was a good boyfriend in other ways, then why leave him because of his thin legs?"

"Perhaps she felt that she wanted to laugh whenever she saw his legs," suggested Constance. "That would not have made him happy. Men do not like to be laughed at. Men do not think they are funny."

This made Mma Ramotswe smile. "That is very amusing! Men do not think they are funny! That is very true, Mma. Very true. You must not laugh at a man, or he will go and hide away like a village dog."

"But there is a serious point," said Kokotso. "Can you call a man good-looking if he has a handsome face but very short legs? I have known men like that. They are good-looking when they are sitting down, but when they stand up and you see how short their legs are you think Oh my God, these are short, short legs!"

"And sometimes, have you noticed," Constance interjected, "have you noticed how men's legs go out at the knees and make a circle? Have you seen that? That is very funny. I always want to laugh when I see men like that."

Kokotso now lowered herself off the wall and began to walk in a circle, her arms hanging loose, her chin stuck out. "This is how men walk," she said. "Have you seen it? They walk like this, almost like monkeys."

It was difficult not to laugh, and if she had thought that these girls seriously entertained this low opinion of men she would have frowned instead, but she knew that these were girls who liked men, a great deal, and so joined Constance in shrieking with laughter at Kokotso's imitation of . . . of the apprentices! How accurate she was, and she did not even know them. To imitate one young man of that sort, then, was to imitate them all.

Kokotso resumed her seat on the wall and for a moment there was silence. Mma Ramotswe was rather surprised at herself, sitting there on a wall with two young women less than half her age, talking about good-looking men. She had seen them when she had driven past the Radio Gabs station at lunch-time, not intending to call in until later that afternoon, but realising that this was exactly the opportunity she was looking for. So she had parked the tiny white van round the corner and had walked back, casually, as one who was spending the lunch hour in a quiet ramble. She had stopped at the entrance to the car park and had gone up to the girls to ask them if they knew the correct time. From there it had been easy. The question about the time had been followed by a remark on how tiring it was to have to walk all the way into town and would they mind if she sat on the wall with them for a few minutes while she summoned up her energy?

Of course she had suspected that these girls were not sitting on the wall just because it was any wall. This was the Radio Gabs wall, and these young ladies were watching the entrance to the radio station. And if one were to ask oneself why girls like this would be watching the entrance to the radio station, it was surely not to see who went in, but who came out. And amongst those who were likely to come out, in terms of good looks and general interest to fashion-conscious girls of seventeen or so, who could it be but Mr Spokes Spokesi, the well-known disc-jockey and radio personality? Spokes Spokesi's show, which stretched from nine in the morning until one-thirty in the afternoon, *Cool Time with Spokes*, was a favourite of younger people in Gaborone. The apprentices listened to it while they were working—although Mr J.L.B. Matekoni, when he could bear it no longer, would switch off their radio in a gesture of defiance. He at least had good taste and a limited tolerance for the inane patter which such radio stations pumped out with great enthusiasm. Mma Ramotswe would have had a similar lack of interest in Spokes except for one thing: he was the second name on the list of Mma Holonga's suitors, unlikely though that was, and this meant that she would have to speak to him at some stage.

"Do you listen to this station?" she asked casually.

Constance clapped her hands. "All the time! All the time! It's the best station there is. The latest music, the latest everything, and . . ."

"And Spokes, of course," supplied Kokotso. "Spokes!"

Mma Ramotswe pretended to look blank. "Spokes? Who is this Spokes? Is he a band?"

Kokotso laughed. "Oh, Mma, you're out of touch. Spokes does a show—the best show you can listen to. Can he talk! Oh my! You hear him talking about music and you can just see him sitting there in front of the mike. Oh!"

"And is he good-looking too?" asked Mma Ramotswe.

"He's fabulous," said Constance. "The best-looking man in Gaborone."

"In all Botswana," suggested Kokotso.

"My!" said Mma Ramotswe. "And will we see him if we sit here long enough? Will we see him coming out?"

"Yes," said Constance. "We come here once a week usually just to see Spokes. He talks to us sometimes; sometimes he just waves. He thinks that we work in that building over there and are just sitting here to pass the lunch hour. He doesn't know that we come to see him."

Mma Ramotswe tried to look intrigued. "How old is this Spokes?" she asked.

"Just the right age," said Constance. "He's twenty-eight. And his birthday is . . ."

"The twenty-fourth of July," said Kokotso. "We shall come here on that day with a present for him. He will like that."

"You are very kind," said Mma Ramotswe. She studied the girls for a moment, trying to imagine what it must be like to worship somebody who was, after all, almost a stranger to them. Why did people behave this way with entertainers? What was so special about them? And then she stopped, for she had remembered Note Mokoti and her own feelings for him all those years ago when she was hardly older than these girls. And the memory made her humble; for we should not forget what it is to be young and to have ideas and attitudes that may later seem so fanciful.

"Will he be out soon?" she asked. "Will we have to wait long?"

"It depends," said Constance. "Sometimes he sits inside and talks to the station manager for hours. But on other days he comes out the moment his show goes off the air and he gets into his car. That is his car over there, that red one with the yellow curtains in the back. It is a very smart car."

Mma Ramotswe glanced at the car. First Class Motors, she thought dismissively, but then Kokotso grabbed her arm and Constance whispered in her ear: Spokes!

He came out of the front door, dressed in his hip-hugging jeans, his shirt open to the third button down, a gold chain round his neck; Spokes Spokesi himself, Gaborone icon, silver-tongued rider of the airwaves, good-looking, confident, ice-cool, flashing white teeth.

"Spokes!" murmured Kokotso, and as if he had heard her barely articulated prayer, he turned in their direction, waved, and began to make his way over the car park to where they sat.

"Hiya, girls! Dumela and all the rest of it, etcetera, etcetera, etcetera!"

Kokotso dug Mma Ramotswe in the ribs. "He's coming to speak to us," she whispered. "He's seen us!"

"Hallo there, Spokes," called out Constance. "Your show today was great. Fantastic. That band you played at ten o'clock. To die for!"

"Yes," said Spokes, who was now standing before them, smiling his devastating smile. "Good sound. A good sound."

"This lady hasn't listened to you yet, Spokes," said Kokotso, gesturing towards Mma Ramotswe. "Now she knows. She'll be listening tomorrow morning, won't you, Mma."

Mma Ramotswe smiled. She did not like to lie and would not lie now. "No," she said. "I won't be listening."

Spokes looked at her quizzically. "Why not, Mma? My music's wrong for you? Is that it? Maybe I can play some more oldies."

"That would be nice," said Mma Ramotswe politely. "But please don't worry about me. You play what your listeners want to hear. I'll be all right."

"I like to please everybody," said Spokes agreeably. "Radio Gabs is for everyone."

"And everyone listens, Spokes," said Kokotso. "You know we listen."

"What are you doing today, Spokes?" asked Constance.

Spokes winked at her. "You know I'd like to take you to the movies, but I have to go and look after the cattle. Sorry about that."

They all laughed at this witticism, Mma Ramotswe included. Then Mma Ramotswe spoke.

"Haven't I seen you before, Rra?" she said, looking at him closely, as if inspecting him. "I'm sure that I've seen you."

Spokes drew back slightly, but seemed bemused. "You see me here and there. Gaborone is not a big place. You might have seen my picture in the papers."

Mma Ramotswe looked doubtful. "No, it wasn't in the papers. No . . ." She paused, as if trying to drag something out of her memory, and then continued, "Yes! That's it. I remember now. I've seen you with that lady who owns the hair-braiding salons. You know the one. I've seen you with her somewhere or other. A party maybe. You were with her. Is she your girlfriend, Rra?"

Her remark made, she watched its effect on him. The easy smile disappeared, and in its place there was a look of anxiety. He glanced at the young girls, who were looking at him eagerly. "Oh that lady! She is my aunty! She is not my girlfriend!"

The girls giggled, and Spokes leaned forward to touch Kokotso lightly on the shoulder. "Meet you later?" he asked. "Metro Club?"

Kokotso squirmed with pleasure. "We'll be there."

"Good," said Spokes, and then, to Mma Ramotswe, "Nice meeting you, aunty. Go carefully."

*   *   *

MMA MAKUTSI listened intently to what Mma Ramotswe had to say when she returned that afternoon from her meeting with Constance, Kokotso, and Spokes.

"I have spent two days on this matter so far," said Mma Ramotswe. "I have met and interviewed two of the suitors on Mma Holonga's list, and neither of them is in the slightest bit suitable. Both can only be interested in her money. One by his own admission—he said it himself, Mma—and the other by the way he behaved."

"Poor Mma Holonga," said Mma Makutsi. "I have read that it is not easy being rich. I have read that you can never tell who is really interested in you or who is interested only in your money."

Mma Ramotswe agreed. "I am going to have to speak to her soon and tell her what progress I have made. I am going to have to say that the first two are definitely unsuitable."

"That is very sad," said Mma Makutsi, thinking how sad it was, too, that there was Mma Holonga with four suitors and there was she with none.

CHAPTER EIGHTEEN

THE PARACHUTE JUMP, AND A
UNIVERSAL TRUTH ABOUT THE
GIVING AND TAKING OF ADVICE

MMA RAMOTSWE was hoping that Mma Potokwane would forget all about the parachute jump which Charlie, the older apprentice, had agreed to take over from Mr J.L.B. Matekoni. Unfortunately, neither Mma Potokwane nor Charlie himself forgot, and indeed Charlie had actively been seeking sponsorship. People were generous; a parachute jump was a considerably more exciting project than a sponsored walk or run—anybody could do those. A parachute jump required courage and there was always the possibility that it could go badly wrong. This made it difficult to refuse a donation.

The jump was planned for a Saturday. The plane would take off from the airport, out near the ostrich abattoir, would circle the town and would then fly out towards Tlokweng and the orphan farm. At the appropriate moment the apprentice would be given the signal to jump and would land, it was hoped, in a large field at the edge of the orphan farm. All the children would be there, waiting to see the parachute come down, and the ranks of the children would be swelled by several press photographers, an official from the Mayor's office—the Mayor himself would be away at the time—a colonel from the Botswana Defence Force

(invited by Mr J.L.B. Matekoni) and the Principal of the Botswana Secretarial College (invited by Mma Makutsi). Mma
Ramotswe had invited Dr Moffat, and had asked him whether he
could possibly bring his medical bag with him—just in case anything went wrong, which she was certain it would not. She had
also invited Mma Holonga, not only because she was something
of a public figure who might be expected to attend a charity event
as a matter of course, but also because she wanted to speak to
her. Apart from these people, the public at large could attend, if it
wished. The event had been given wide publicity in the papers,
and even Spokes Spokesi had mentioned it on his show on Radio
Gabs. He claimed to have done a parachute jump himself, and
that it was nothing, "as long as you were brave enough." But
things could go wrong, he warned, although he did not propose to
say anything more on that subject just then.

Charlie himself seemed very calm. On the day before the
jump, Mma Ramotswe had a private word with him at the garage,
telling him that there would be no dishonour in his withdrawing,
even at this late stage.

"Nobody will think the less of you if you phone Mma Potokwane right now and tell her that you have changed your mind.
Nobody will think that you are a coward."

"Yes, they will," said Charlie. "And anyway, I want to do it. I
have been practising and I know everything there is to know
about parachutes now. You count ten—or is it fifty?—and then
you pull the cord. So. Like that. Then you keep your feet together
and you roll over on the ground once you land. That is all there is
to it."

Mma Ramotswe wanted to say that it was not so simple, but
she kept her own counsel.

"You could come with me, Mma Ramotswe," said Charlie,
jokingly. "They could make an extra big parachute for you."

Mma Ramotswe ignored this. He could be right, of course; perhaps you needed an especially large parachute if you were of traditional build, or perhaps you just came down faster. But then parachutists of traditional build would land more softly and comfortably, being better padded, and those of particularly traditional build might just roll over when they landed, as barrels do when you drop them.

"Well," she said, after a while, "in your case you must be hoping to land on your bottom, which is much bigger than normal. That will be the best place for you to land. Put your feet up when you get close to the ground and sit down."

The apprentice looked annoyed, but he did not say anything. Instead, he looked in a small mirror which he had hung on a pin near the door that led from the garage into the office. He could often be found standing before this mirror, preening himself, or doing a small, shuffling dance while he looked at his reflection.

ON THE day in question, they all met at Tlokweng Road Speedy Motors: Mma Ramotswe; the two children, Motholeli and Puso; Mr J.L.B. Matekoni; Mma Makutsi; and the younger apprentice. Charlie himself had been collected from his home several hours earlier and driven to the airfield by the pilot of the light aircraft from which he was to jump.

They drove out to the orphan farm in Mma Ramotswe's tiny white van and in Mr J.L.B. Matekoni's truck, Mma Makutsi travelling in the van with Mma Ramotswe and the children sitting in the back. Motholeli's wheelchair was secured in the back of the van by a system of ropes which Mr J.L.B. Matekoni had devised, and this gave her a very good view of the passing countryside. People waved to her, and she waved back, "like the Queen," she said. Mma Ramotswe had told her all about the Queen Elizabeth and about how she had been a friend of Sir Seretse Khama himself. She loved Botswana, explained Mma Ramotswe, and she did her duty all the time, all the time, visiting people and shaking their hands and being given flowers by children. She had been on duty for fifty years, Mma Ramotswe said, just like Mr Mandela, who had given his whole life for justice and had never once thought of himself. How unlike these people were modern politicians, who thought only of power and tricks.

By the time they drew up at the orphan farm, the trees outside the office already had cars under them, and they were obliged to leave the tiny white van out on the road. People had obviously already begun to arrive, and some of the children were on duty at the gate, standing smartly and greeting the guests, telling them where they should go for tea and cake before the jump took place. Some of the younger children were wearing cardboard aeroplane badges which they had cut out and coloured themselves, and some of these were on sale for two pula at a small table under a tree.

Mma Potokwane saw them from her office, and she rushed out to meet them just as Mr J.L.B. Matekoni and the younger apprentice arrived in the truck. Then Dr Moffat arrived, with his wife, in his pick-up truck, and Mma Potokwane immediately seized him and led him off to look at one of the children who had developed a high fever and was being watched over by her housemother. Mrs Moffat stayed with Mma Ramotswe and Mma Makutsi and together they made their way to the spot under a wide jacaranda tree where two of the housemothers were dispensing heavily-sugared tea from a very large brown tea-pot. There was cake too, but it was not free. Mma Ramotswe bought a slice for all of them and they sat down on stools and drank the tea and ate the cake while further spectators arrived. Then, after half an hour or so, they heard the distant drone of an aircraft engine and the children began to squeal with excitement, pointing at the sky to the west. Mma Ramotswe looked up, straining her eyes; the sound was clear enough now, and yes, there it was, a small plane, white against the great empty sky, much higher than she had imagined it would be. How small we must all look from up there, she thought; and poor Charlie, for all his faults, now just a tiny dot in the sky, a tiny dot that would come tumbling down to the hard earth below.

"I shouldn't have asked him to do this," she said to Mma Makutsi. "What if he's killed?"

Mma Makutsi put a reassuring hand on Mma Ramotswe's forearm. "He won't be," she said. "These things are very safe these days. They check everything two or three times."

"But it still might not open. And what if he freezes with shock and doesn't pull the cord? What then?"

"His instructor will be jumping with him," soothed Mma Makutsi. "He would dive down and pull the cord for him. I saw a picture in the *National Geographic* of that being done. It is very easy for these people."

They became silent as the plane passed overhead. Now they could see the markings underneath the wings and the undercarriage, and then the opening door and a figure and a blur of shapes. Suddenly there were two little packages, but packages with arms and legs flailing about in the rushing wind, and some of the children shrieked and pointed upwards. Mr J.L.B. Matekoni looked up too, and gulped, imagining that it could have been him up there, and remembering that disturbing dream. Mma Ramotswe closed her eyes, and then opened them again, and still the figures were falling against the empty sky, and she thought: his parachute is not going to open, and she clutched at Mma Makutsi who had muttered something under her breath, a prayer perhaps.

But the parachutes did open, and Mma Ramotswe let out her

breath and felt weak at the knees. Mrs Moffat smiled at her and said, "I was worried then. It seemed such a time," and Mma Ramotswe was too overcome to say anything in response, but vowed to herself that she would make it up to this boy in the future; she would be kind to him and not be so impatient at the irritating things he said and did.

As they drifted down, floating beneath the great white canopies, the two figures separated. One of them waved to the other, and seemed to be gesturing, but the other did nothing and continued to float away. The gesturing one was now getting fairly close to the ground, and within seconds he had landed in the field, scarcely a few hundred yards from the spectators. There was a cheer, and the children ran forward, in spite of the calls from the housemothers to stay where they were until the second parachutist had landed safely.

They need not have worried. The other parachutist, now revealed to be Charlie, had so drifted off course that he did not land in the field at all, but disappeared behind the tree tops of the scrub bush on the other side. The spectators watched silently as this happened, and then people turned to one another in uncertainty.

"He will be dead," cried out one of the smaller children. "We must fetch a box."

IT WAS Mr J.L.B. Matekoni, Mma Potokwane's husband, and the instructor (not freed of his equipment) who discovered Charlie. He was hanging a few feet above the ground, his parachute covering the upper branches of a large acacia tree, snagged and snared by the thorny limbs of the tree. He shouted out to them as they approached, and the instructor soon had him out of the harness and down on the ground.

"That was a soft landing," said the instructor. "Well done. You were just a bit off target, that's all. I think you were pulling on the wrong side of the canopy. That's why you sailed off here."

The apprentice nodded. He had a curious expression on his face, half way between sheer relief and pain.

"I think that I am injured," he said.

"You can't be," said the instructor, dusting down the green parachute suit. "The tree completely broke your fall."

The apprentice shook his head. "There is something hurting me. It is very sore. It is there. Please see what it is."

Mr J.L.B. Matekoni looked at the seat of Charlie's trousers. There was a large rip in the fabric and a very nasty-looking acacia thorn, several inches long, embedded in the flesh. Deftly he took this between his fingers and extracted it with one swift move-ment. The apprentice gave a yelp.

"That was all," said Mr J.L.B. Matekoni. "A big thorn . . ."

"Please do not tell them," said the apprentice. "Please do not tell them where it was."

"Of course I will not," said Mr J.L.B. Matekoni. "You are a brave, brave young man."

The apprentice smiled. He was recovering from his shock now. "Are the newspaper people there?" he asked. "Did they come?"

"They are there," said Mma Potokwane's husband. "And many girls too."

Back under the trees he received a hero's welcome. The chil-dren ran round him, tugging at his sleeves, the housemothers fussed over him with mugs of tea and large slices of cake, and the girls looked on admiringly. Charlie basked in the glory of it all, smiling at the photographers when they approached with their cameras, and patting children on the head, just as an experienced hero might do. Mma Ramotswe watched with amusement, and considerable relief, and then went off to talk to Mma Holonga, whom she had spotted arriving rather late, when the jump had already taken place. She took her client a mug of tea and led her to a private place under a tree, where they could both sit in privacy and talk.

"I have started making enquiries for you," she began. "I have spoken to two of the men on your list and I can give you a report on what I have found out so far."

Mma Holonga nodded. "Well, yes. I must say that there have been developments since I saw you. But tell me anyway. Then I shall tell you what I have decided to do."

Mma Ramotswe could not conceal her surprise. What was the point of consulting her if Mma Holonga was going to make a decision before receiving even a preliminary report?

"You've decided something?" she asked.

"Yes," said Mma Holonga, in a matter-of-fact voice. "But you go ahead and tell me what you found out. I'm very interested."

Mma Ramotswe began her account. "A few days ago I met your Mr Spokesi," she said. "I had a conversation with him and in the course of this conversation I realised that he was not being honest with you. He is a man who likes younger ladies and I do not think that he is serious about marrying you. I think that he would like to have a good time using your money, and then he would go back to the other ladies. I'm sorry about that, Mma, but there it is."

"Of course," said Mma Holonga, tossing back her head. "That man is very vain and is interested only in himself. I think I knew that all along. You have confirmed my views, Mma."

Mma Ramotswe was slightly taken aback by this. She had expected a measure of disappointment on Mma Holonga's part, an expression of regret, instead of which Mr Spokes Spokesi, who must have been a lively suitor, was being consigned to oblivion quite insouciantly.

"Then there is the teacher," Mma Ramotswe went on. "Mr Bobologo. He is a much more serious man than that Spokesi person. He is a clever man, I think; very well-read."

Mma Holonga smiled. "Yes," she said. "He is a good man."

"But a very dull one too," said Mma Ramotswe. "And he is interested only in getting hold of your money to use for his House of Hope. That is all that interests him. I think that . . ."

Mma Ramotswe tailed off. Her words were having a strange effect on Mma Holonga, she thought. Her client was now sitting bolt upright, her lips pursed in disapproval of what Mma Ramotswe was telling her.

"That is not true!" Mma Holonga expostulated. "He would never do a thing like that."

Mma Ramotswe sighed. "I am sorry, Mma. In my job I often have to tell people things that they do not want to hear. I think that you might not want to hear what I have to say, but I must say it nonetheless. That is my duty. That man is after your money."

Mma Holonga stared at Mma Ramotswe. She rose to her feet, dusting at her skirts as she did so. "You have been very good, Mma," she said coldly. "I am very grateful to you for finding out about Spokesi. Oh yes, you have done well there. But when it comes to my fiancé, Mr Bobologo, you must stop talking about him in this way. I have decided to marry him, and that is it."

Mma Ramotswe did not know what to say and for a few moments she struggled with herself. Clovis Andersen, as far as she could remember, had never written about what to do in this precise situation and she was thrown back on first principles. There was her duty to her client, which was to carry out the enquiries which she had been asked to conduct. But then there was her duty to warn—a simple human duty which involved warning somebody of danger which they were courting. That duty existed, of course, but at the same time one should not be paternalistic and interfere in matters in which another person wished to choose for themselves. It was not for Mma Ramotswe to make Mma Holonga's decisions for her.

She decided to be cautious. "Are you sure about this, Mma?" she asked. "I hope that you do not think I am being rude in asking, but are you sure that you wish to marry this man? It is a very major decision."

Mma Holonga seemed to be pacified by Mma Ramotswe's tone, and she smiled as she replied. "Well, Mma, you are right about its being a very major decision. I am well aware of that. But I have decided that my destiny lies with that man."

"And you know all about his . . . his interests?"

"You mean his good works? His work for others?"

"The House of Hope. The bar girls . . ."

Mma Holonga looked out over the orphan farm field, as if searching for bar girls. "I know all about that. In fact, I am very much involved in that good work. Since I came to see you, he has shown me the House of Hope and I have been doing work there. I have started hair-braiding classes for those bad girls and then they can come and work in my salons."

"That is a very good idea," said Mma Ramotswe. "And then there is the possible extension . . ."

"That too," interrupted Mma Holonga. "I shall be paying for that. I have already talked to a builder I know. Then, after that is done, I am going to build a House of Hope out at Molepolole, for bad girls from that region. That was all my idea, not Bobologo's."

Mma Ramotswe listened to all this and realised that she was in the presence of a woman who had found her vocation. So there was nothing more for her to say, other than to congratulate her on her forthcoming marriage and to reflect on the truth that when people ask for advice they very rarely want your advice and will go ahead and do what they want to do anyway, no matter what you say. That applied in every sort of case; it was a human truth of universal application, but one which most people knew little or nothing about.

CHAPTER NINETEEN

A VERY RICH CAKE IS SERVED

AFTER SHE had finished her surprising discussion with Mma Holonga, Mma Ramotswe moved over to join Mr J.L.B. Matekoni and Mma Makutsi, who were sitting at a table under a tree near the children's dining room. More tea had been produced and was being served by the housemothers, and Mma Ramotswe noticed that there were many people in the crowd whom she knew. Indeed, some of them were relatives of hers; her cousin and husband, for example, and some of Mr J.L.B. Matekoni's people. Mma Potokwane had obviously been very active in gathering people for the parachute drop.

She walked over to join her cousin, who said that she would not be prepared to do a parachute drop, even if asked by the President himself. "I would have to say, I'm sorry Rra, but there are some things one cannot do, even for Botswana. I cannot jump from an aeroplane. I would die straightaway."

The cousin's husband agreed. He would be prepared to give all his money, and all his cattle, to charity rather than jump.

"You should not let Mma Potokwane hear that," said Mma Ramotswe. "It might give her ideas."

Then there was a conversation with the Reverend Trevor

Mwamba from the Anglican Cathedral. He, too, confessed that he would not like to do a parachute jump, and he felt that the same could be said for the Bishop. For a moment Mma Ramotswe entertained a mental picture of the Bishop jumping from an aeroplane, dressed in his episcopal robes and clutching his mitre as he fell.

"It is nothing, you know," said Charlie, who had come up to join them, a glass of beer in his hand, and clearly enjoying his fame. "I wasn't at all frightened. I just jumped and then bump! the chute opened above me and I came down. That's all there is to it. I will do it again tomorrow if Mma Potokwane asks me. In fact, I think I might offer to join the Botswana Defence Force. I could look after their aeroplane engines and then do some jumping in my spare time."

Mma Ramotswe saw that this made Mr J.L.B. Matekoni look anxious, but the conversation moved on to another topic and no more was said of the looking-after of aeroplane engines.

The event had now turned into something of a party. Some of the older children, who had been helping with the tea cups and with arranging chairs under the trees, now formed up as a choir and sang several songs while one of them, a talented marimba player, provided an accompaniment. Then, after the singing, Mma Potokwane came over to Mma Ramotswe's side and invited her to join her for a moment in the office. The same invitation was extended to Mr J.L.B. Matekoni, and it was explained that a very special cake had been prepared for him but that it could not be produced in public as there was not enough for everybody.

They went into the office. The Reverend Trevor Mwamba was already there, a plate of cake before him. He stood up and smiled at Mr J.L.B. Matekoni.

"Now," said Mma Potokwane, putting a large slice of the special cake on Mr J.L.B. Matekoni's plate. "Here is the special cake I have made."

"You are very kind to us, Mma," said Mr J.L.B. Matekoni. "This looks like a very rich cake. Very rich." He paused, the cake half way to his mouth. He looked at Mma Potokwane. Then he looked at the Reverend Trevor Mwamba. Finally he looked at Mma Ramotswe. Nobody spoke.

Mma Potokwane broke the silence. "Mr J.L.B. Matekoni," she said. "We all know how proud you are of Mma Ramotswe. We all know how proud you are to be her fiancé and how you wish to be her husband. I am right, am I not, in saying that you wish to be her husband?"

Mr J.L.B. Matekoni nodded. "I do. Of course I do."

"Well, do you not think that the moment has come?" she went on. "Do you not think that this would be the right time to marry Mma Ramotswe? Right now. Not next month or next year or whenever, but right now. Because if you do not do something about this, you may never do it. Life is perilous. At any time it could be too late. When you love another person, you must tell her, but you must also show her. You must do that thing that says to the world that you love that person. And this must never be put off, never."

She paused, watching the effect of her words on Mr J.L.B. Matekoni. He was staring at her, his eyes slightly moist, as if he was about to burst into tears.

"You do wish to marry Mma Ramotswe, do you not?" Mma Potokwane urged.

Now there was a further silence. The Reverend Trevor Mwamba slipped a small piece of cake into his mouth and chewed on it. Mma Ramotswe herself looked down at the ground, at the edge of Mma Potokwane's carpet. And then Mr J.L.B. Matekoni spoke.

"I will marry Mma Ramotswe right now," he said. "If that is what Mma Ramotswe wishes, then I shall do that. I shall be proud to do that. There is no other lady I would ever wish to marry. Just Mma Ramotswe. That is all."

It was a long speech for Mr J.L.B. Matekoni, but every word was filled with passion and a new determination.

"In that case," said the Reverend Trevor Mwamba, wiping the crumbs from the edge of his lips. "In that case I have the prayer books in my car and I have the Bishop's authority to perform the ceremony right here."

"We can do it under the big tree," said Mma Potokwane. "I will tell the children's choir to get ready. And I will also tell the guests to prepare themselves. They will be surprised."

THEY ASSEMBLED under the boughs of the great jacaranda tree. A table had been covered with a clean white sheet and served as an altar, and before this altar stood Mr J.L.B. Matekoni, waiting for Mma Ramotswe to be led up to him by Mma Potokwane's husband, who had offered to give the bride away on behalf of her late father, Obed Ramotswe. Mma Potokwane had produced a suitable dress for Mma Ramotswe, in just the right size as it happened, and Mr J.L.B. Matekoni had been put into a suit by Mma Potokwane's husband. The Reverend Trevor Mwamba had fetched his robes from his car.

When Mma Ramotswe came out of the office and walked with Mma Potokwane's husband up to the group of people and the waiting groom, there were enthusiastic ululations from the crowd. This was how people showed their delight and pleasure and the sound was strong that day.

"Dearly beloved," began the Reverend Trevor Mwamba, "we are gathered here together in the sight of God and in the presence of this congregation to join this man and this woman in holy matrimony, which is an honourable estate . . ."

The words which Mma Ramotswe had heard so many times for others, those echoing words, she now heard for herself, and she made the responses clearly, as did Mr J.L.B. Matekoni. Then, taking their hands and placing them together, in accordance with the authority vested in him, the Reverend Trevor Mwamba pronounced them man and wife, and the ladies present, led by Mma Potokwane, ululated with pleasure.

The choir had been waiting, and now they sang, while Mma Ramotswe and Mr J.L.B. Matekoni sat down on chairs which had been placed before the altar, and signed the register which the Reverend Trevor Mwamba had also happened to have in the back of his car. The choir sang, the sweet voices of the children rising through the branches of the tree above them, and filling the still, clear air with sound. There was an old Botswana hymn, one which everybody knew, and then, because it was a favourite of Mma Ramotswe's father, they sang that song which distils all the suffering and the hope of Africa; that song which had inspired and comforted so many, "Nkosi Sikeleli Afrika," God Bless Africa, give her life, watch over her children.

Mma Ramotswe turned to face her friends, and smiled, and they smiled back. Then she and Mr J.L.B. Matekoni stood up and walked down through the crowd to the place where the children had taken more tables and where, quite miraculously, as at Cana of Galilee, the housemothers had set out large plates of food, ready for the wedding feast.

ABOUT THE AUTHOR

Alexander McCall Smith is a professor of medical law at Edinburgh University. He was born in what is now known as Zimbabwe and taught law at the University of Botswana. He is the author of more than fifty books: novels, stories, children's books, and specialized titles such as *Forensic Aspects of Sleep*. He lives in Scotland.